THE BARNACLE'S SON

THE PALE CHRONICLES
BOOK TWO

LEN BOSWELL

Black Rose Writing | Texas

ISBN: 978-1-68513-230-9
PUBLISHED BY BLACK ROSE WRITING
www.blackrosewriting.com

Printed in the United States of America
Suggested Retail Price (SRP) $20.95

The Barnacle's Son is printed in Book Antiqua

*As a planet-friendly publisher, Black Rose Writing does its best to eliminate unnecessary waste to reduce paper usage and energy costs, while never compromising the reading experience. As a result, the final word count vs. page count may not meet common expectations.

OTHER BOOKS BY LEN BOSWELL

Fantasies:
Barnum's Angel
The Cave of the Six Arrows
The Fool's Gambit

Simon Grave Mysteries:
A Grave Misunderstanding
Simon Grave and the Curious Incident of the Cat in the Daytime
Simon Grave and the Drone of the Basque Orvilles
Simon Grave and the Sons of Irony
Simon Grave and the School of Casual Invisibility
Simon Grave and the Wrath of Grapes

Other Mysteries:
Flicker: A Paranormal Mystery
Skeleton: A Bare Bones Mystery
Penelope Goodlove's Invisible Detective Agency: The Elephant Who Cried Wolf

Novellas:
LIQ: The Quality of Mercy

Memoirs:
Santa Takes a Tumble
Unboxing Raymond

Nonfiction:
The Leadership Secrets of Squirrels
Stick Figures: The Life and Art of Len Boswell

THE
BARNACLE'S
SON

"This renowned monster, who had come off victorious in a hundred fights with his pursuers, was an old bull whale, of prodigious size and strength. From the effect of age, or more probably from a freak of nature . . . *he was white as wool!* . . . Viewed from a distance, the practised eye of the sailor only could decide, that the moving mass . . . was not a white cloud sailing along the horizon. On the spermaceti whale, barnacles are rarely discovered; but upon the head of this *lusus naturae,* they had clustered, until it became absolutely rugged with the shells."
—**Jeremiah Reynolds,** *Mocha Dick: Or The White Whale of the Pacific, Knickerbocker Magazine,* **May 1839**

"Mystery surrounds the Sixth Voyage of the Treasure Fleet of Emperor Zhu Di. Some scholars of repute say that the junks, numbering 200, never sailed beyond the South China Sea, the Indian Ocean, and the Arabian Sea. Others suggest that the fleet, numbering 100 ships, split into four groups, each accompanied by 'future dragons of the empire.' One of the groups, led by Admiral Zhou Man, sailed through what would later be called the Straits of Magellan, losing seven junks, including the egg of a white dragon, before heading up the coast of Peru and then visiting Canada, New Zealand, and Australia. The fanciful inclusion of dragons makes this second interpretation suspect, and reminds this historian of the utmost importance of parsing fact from myth."
—**John Waterford Snelling,** *Voyages of the Treasure Fleets, 1405-1433*

PROLOGUE

Western Coast of the Isle of Skye, Scotland, May 18, 1421.

Xu Chang, Second Assassin of the Red Dragon and guardian of the green dragon, sat atop the bluff overlooking the crashing waves below. To the west he could see the lanterns of the junk that had delivered him growing dimmer and dimmer in the darkness.

After so many months at sea, he had found it difficult to walk on firm land, let alone clamber up the bluff with two heavy sacks, one containing the egg of the green dragon, the other his collection of small Shaolin weapons: an iron pen, three hand darts, a thorn, a nine-section whip, and an iron flute. His only large weapon, a staff, lay at his side.

He looked to the east, where the sun was trying to rise above a mountain. If you could call it a mountain. It had rocky spires like Mount Song, where he had been trained by the Shaolin Monks along the Yellow River, but it was too low, no more than a large hill compared to Mount Song or any of The Five Great Mountains, which were three times as high.

He ran his hand through the thick dewy grass — if indeed it was grass — pulled up a handful, and brought it to his nose. Fragrant, sweet, a flower of some kind perhaps, but unlike anything he had smelled before. Everything he saw or touched was familiar and yet strange, as if the gods had given reality a slight twist.

He started to stand, then sat back down quickly. Four torches were bouncing along the hillside, no more than a spear throw away. He flattened himself against the ground, hoping his green clothing would blend in.

After a minute, he raised his head to look for the torches. They had moved off to the south. He collected his sacks, grabbed his staff, and stood, looking in all directions. Nothing.

The sky was growing lighter. He would have to walk quickly to the east, to find safety in the mountains, at least for a time. His pale eyes could not withstand the assault of the morning sun, even with the protection provided by his wide-brimmed hat, made from green reeds gathered from a marsh near the Yellow River.

So it begins, he thought. *This land. This life. My duty. My dragon. Wherever the path leads.*

PART ONE

"The Emperor did a treasure fleet build, the junks in colours glorious and numbering twice a hundred, led by his admirals four, with crews proud and brave, each flagship carrying a single secret cargo beneath the waterline, in a net secure, dragon eggs fresh but ready to birth in distant lands, their territory to secure, safely away from his dying dragons, all laid low by a malady without cure. Stories are many, of bravery, of mystery, of calamity at sea. No dragons returned, stories and dragons passing into myth. But listen yet. . . ."

– Zhang Wei, *The Emperor's Dragons* (1513)

1

British Geological Survey, Nottingham, October 14, Present Day.

Bruce Cargo had had just about enough, his hands shaking with anger as his boss, Dr. Shepherd, not so affectionately known as "Old Nozzle," turned and walked away.

Clean up the gloomy corner, he had said. *Today.*

Bruce's first thought was to quietly pack his things and leave a brief note of resignation for the bastard. *Fuck that, I'm a scientist, not an intern.*

But then he had had second thoughts, the most compelling being the desire to keep his job. If he botched this opportunity, he'd probably have to go back to the States, and he didn't want that. And there was Luna to consider. She would not think kindly if he blew this, perhaps his last chance to grab a foothold on any semblance of a career, at least in England.

So he had calmed himself and set about the task, yanking off his tie, rolling up his sleeves, and arming himself with a flashlight, a makeshift dust cloth, and a bottle of water from the machine.

At five foot ten, he was not a big man, but he was athletic, with broad shoulders, well-defined muscles, and the obligatory six-pack abs of a devoted gym rat. Not many people would have called him handsome, but there was something about him that attracted women, who invariably called him sexy, noting his square jaw, long sandy hair, and ice blue eyes. Rugged good looks, they would say, an aura about him.

The first two hours had been exactly what he had expected: a cloud of dust, the smell of mildew and aging samples and slides, and myriad boxes and other containers to sort through and rearrange into like categories, butterflies here, small mammal bones there, and so on.

And then he had happened upon a small barrel, sealed top and bottom to protect the specimens inside from a sea voyage, but broken open nonetheless, and in a strange way. At first he thought that someone had hit the side of the barrel hard with an ax, but it was soon apparent that the force had come from *inside* the barrel, not outside, the wood bursting outward. Stranger still, there were no splinters or wood chips on the floor around the barrel, indicating that perhaps the barrel had been moved to the gloomy corner after whatever burst out had burst out.

He peered into the opening in the barrel and pulled out fragments of a modest-sized egg encrusted with what looked like long-dead barnacles, perhaps an ostrich egg, although the color seemed wrong, and a small package wrapped in sail cloth and tightly bound in hemp twine.

The writing on the package sent a shock through him: *C. Darwin, Esq. Do not open.*

His first thought was to run straight to Old Nozzle with his find, but he quickly reconsidered; he didn't want Old Nozzle to get credit for the find, which he knew would be the case if he quickly turned it over. If he had learned nothing else during his time with the Survey, it was that everything was about Old Nozzle, who insisted on having his hands in everything, no matter how small. So he threw the shell fragments and the package into a garbage bag, slid the barrel back into the corner, turning its jagged opening against the wall, and piled other boxes on top. He would come back for it later, when it was time to involve Old Nozzle and eventually the press.

But first he wanted to find out more about the package. Find some quiet place and open it.

"What are you up to, Bruce?" The voice startled him, making him clutch the garbage bag tighter. He knew it was Jamie Doyle, the scientist from down the hall. There was no mistaking his deep, booming voice. Bruce doubted whether Jamie had a whisper in him.

He turned and stared directly into Jamie's pale face and seemingly red eyes, the signature eyes of a man with albinism. He was taller than Bruce by a head, but stooped, and tended to loom over people in conversation as a way of intimidating them. As always, he was dressed in a smart but baggy 3-piece gray suit, an accommodation for his hunched shoulders, with a solid red tie and matching handkerchief neatly folded into his breast pocket. And always a white shirt. Bruce imagined Jamie's closet filled with rows of these suits and shirts, because his look never varied, even on those occasions where something more, like a tuxedo, would have been more appropriate. He was known throughout the department as "the Man in Gray" or simply "Red." Less kind people referred to him behind his back as "Flaps," a dark homage to the way his expansive unbuttoned suit jacket flapped at his sides like dead wings when he walked briskly down the hall.

Bruce took a step back. "Nothing," he said, his voice noticeably shaky. "Just cleaning up a bit for Old Nozzle."

"Really? I doubt anyone's waded through this junk in thirty years."

"Well, there's certainly some old stuff, unregistered specimens, mostly spoiled, from as far back as the 1820s. A few good slides from Hooker and Henslow that may be of interest. How they ended up here, I don't know."

"Probably by way of the old geology museum in South Kensington would be my guess. Maybe even from the old Piccadilly museum."

"At any rate," said Bruce, shaking the garbage bag, his voice quavering, "most not worth the storage space. Already on my fifth bag."

Jamie squinted at him and then glanced around the room. "Why are you so nervous?"

Bruce tried to calm himself. "Nervous? No, it's pure anger, I guess. I mean, why should I get stuck with this mess, especially with a report overdue?"

Jamie stared at him intently, forcing Bruce to look away.

"Now, if you'll excuse me," said Bruce, "I have to finish up some *real* work before the end of the day. If I don't get my report done, I'm toast."

Jamie smirked. "Meeting Luna after work, I suppose."

"Of course, it's the weekend." He wasn't looking forward to the long drive into London, especially on a Friday, but seeing Luna would make up for it. And they would be looking for houses this weekend, somewhere in between Nottingham and London, so they could live together every day.

Jamie glowered at him. He hated the fact that Luna, a model with albinism known professionally as Moon Indigo, preferred Bruce over him and had rebuffed him at every opportunity. He was persistent to a fault and took every opportunity to make himself more worthy in her eyes, including his most recent attempt: trying out as a runway model, with no success. His look was "too threatening," they had said.

Bruce pushed by Jamie and headed back to his desk with the garbage bag. Behind him he could hear Jamie poking around at the boxes in the corner.

2

Preston-Manfred Agency, London, October 14.

Luna Fearnow stared at the older gentleman sitting across from her, the third candidate of the day, and perhaps the most promising. He at least had the common sense to arrive in a chauffeur's uniform, pressed and starched, complete with cap and driving gloves, which he pulled from his hands finger by finger at the start of the interview, in perhaps an overly showy way, as if to indicate that he, too, was conducting an interview.

He was fifty or so, short and thin, but with broad shoulders and an air of athleticism about him. His salt-and-pepper hair was buzz cut, perhaps to veil an obviously retreating hairline, or perhaps he was just following the fashion of the day. His features, except for his cobalt blue eyes, were so nondescript anyone passing him on the street would pass him on the street. Except for the uniform, he was almost as good as invisible.

As someone with albinism, she watched for early signs of prejudice, or at least discomfort, and they were usually there every time, and had been with the other applicants this afternoon: a startle response upon first seeing her, a forced smile, excessive blinking, looking away, fascination with her hair to the point of almost reaching out and touching it—all manner of obvious and subtle indicators—but she was sensing none from this man.

"So," she said, fumbling with his one-page resume, "Mr. Pibb, is it?"

"Yes, madam, Pontius Pibb's the name." He glanced around the room, taking in photographs of her on the covers of various fashion magazines. "And you must be Moon Indigo, model of the year."

"Yes and no," she said, glancing up at that old cover photo. "That was *several* years ago, I'm afraid, and my real name is actually Luna Fearnow."

"So . . ."

"Moon Indigo is the clever name they gave me back when I was too young and naïve to object."

"Excuse me, madam, but neither name sounds Swedish."

"Swedish?"

"I mean, you're Swedish, right, or at least Scandinavian?"

"Nope. Born and raised in West Virginia. Scottish by heritage, with a little German thrown in, actually."

"But you're so blond and fair. Remind me of Tilda Swinton, you do."

Luna couldn't help but laugh. "I get that a lot, Mr. Pibb, but actually Tilda Swinton is Scottish as well. And I'm fair not because I'm Swedish or *Swintonish*, but because I have albinism."

Pibb raised an eyebrow. "Blimey, I've never met an albino before."

Luna slapped her hand on the desk, though not hard enough to create much of a sound. "Stop right there, Mr. Pibb. Time for the first rule about *albinos*: never call us that. It's like the N word."

"Truly?"

"Oh, yes."

"Well, my apologies, I meant no offense."

"No offense taken."

"I'll be more careful in future, madam. Speaking of which, is the job still available?"

"Yes, and you're the last person I have to interview."

"So I have a chance?"

"You do."

"Well, I hope Barnes's Law applies over Blick's."

"Excuse me?"

"Oh, sorry, miss. Barnes's Law is there's a fifty percent chance of anything. Either it happens or it doesn't."

"And Blick's Law?"

"Actually, it's Blick's *Rule*: You have two chances, slim and none."

Luna smiled. "Well, I'd say a third law of some kind must be at work, Mr. Pibb. I'd say your chances are *very* good." She set his resume aside. "But first let me describe the job for you. You might just want to walk away."

"Fair enough."

3

British Geological Survey, Nottingham, October 14.

Bruce walked hurriedly down the hall to his office, where he hoped to collect his thoughts about the find and what to do next. The answer was obvious: call Luna. She had a way of cutting through the fog that surrounded any issue to come up with logical solutions.

But as he stepped into his office, he came upon Old Nozzle flipping through a stack of papers on his desk, including a report now six days late. "May I help you, sir?"

Old Nozzle, the staff name for Dr. Ronald Shepherd, was a man with a prominent nose, made more prominent by his small head and short stature. Afflicted by perhaps every allergy known to man, he was forever dealing with a dripping nose. Thus the nickname. He was a good scientist but not a good leader, being more concerned with his own advancement than the needs of his staff.

Old Nozzle continued to leaf through the report, as if snooping was his prerogative, then set it down. "Help me? No, not really. Just curious about what you might have found, if anything, in that gloomy, gloomy corner—disgusting, isn't it?"

Bruce took a deep breath to control his anger, sat down in his guest chair, and slipped the garbage bag under it. "Yes, and no, I didn't find much. A lot of dust and spoiled specimens and slides from the 1820s and 1830s. A decent slide or two by Henslow and Hooker."

Old Nozzle cringed at the word "dust," then raised an eyebrow. "Henslow? Hooker? My, my, I'd like to see those."

"Of course. I'll bring them 'round when I finish up on Monday morning. There may be others."

"What, not finishing today?"

"No, it's slow going, and I have a dental appointment in London this afternoon."

"Really? I don't recall your mentioning that."

Bruce put his hand to his cheek and feigned a grimace. "A toothache, came on suddenly."

Old Nozzle pursed his lips, wondering whether he had just been lied to—a dental appointment on a Friday, in faraway London?—then stood and headed for the door. "I see. Well, then, as soon as possible Monday morning?"

"Yes, of course."

Old Nozzle walked to the door, then turned. "Oh, have you seen the Man in Gray around? He was dead set against my having you clean out that corner. Can't wait to tell him what you found."

"Oh, he knows, sir. He dropped by while I was finishing up for the day. He may still be there, in fact."

"Well, then, I'll chase him down and gloat a bit. And speaking of that, I may need your help on a press release. Give it some thought over the weekend. Henslow and Hooker slides will be big news."

"Of course."

Old Nozzle nodded, blew his nose, and was gone. Bruce pulled out his cell phone and called Luna, who seemed annoyed when she picked up, not even letting him say hello.

"Bruce, I'm in the middle of an interview. I'll call you back." Then she ended the call.

Bruce grabbed the garbage bag and his sports coat and headed for the door. He'd call her again when he got to his apartment.

4

Preston-Manfred Agency, London, October 14.

Pontius Pibb sat there and listened as best he could to the pale, beautiful woman who stood between him and gainful employment. As she described the requirements of the job, all pretty straightforward as far as he could tell—pick her up, take her here, take her there—he studied her. Her beauty certainly was Swintonesque, although she appeared to be younger, perhaps no more than thirty years old or so: a face of angles and smooth surfaces, high cheekbones, broad forehead, hair cropped short, pale beyond platinum and swept back on top, almost like a crewcut but taller, her eyes, sometimes flashing light blue, sometimes pink or purple, her pupils moving rapidly from side to side, as if she were trying to take in the entire room all at once. She was a stunner, no doubt, tall and sleek, with breasts just large enough, a nice handful to his mind, and shapely legs that seemed to go on forever. Her skin, however pale, was wonderfully smooth.

She wasn't dressed the way he expected a fashion model to dress. No outrageous hat, no convolutions of fabric, no dress slit from here to there and beyond, no eight-inch heels, no garish sci-fi makeup. In fact, her way of dressing was decidedly plain: black wool slacks and sensible flats, a white blouse—albeit sporting a sizeable coffee stain — and no makeup or jewelry save for a silver bracelet on her left wrist, which she twisted nervously as she spoke. No watch. No rings. No earrings. And, from what he could tell, no perfume either.

He sensed that she had paused, and quickly looked her in the eye.

"And that's about it, Mr. Pibb. Any questions?"

He loved her voice, which was deeper than the voices of most women he knew, kind of like Stevie Nicks, low and sexy.

"Yes, madam, a couple. Firstly, you've told me what I'll be doing, but not why."

"Why?"

"Yes, why is the position open and why do you even need a chauffeur?"

Luna sighed. This could take a while, and she was eager to get home. "Okay, let's start with the easy part. The job is open because I was previously chauffeured about by a limousine agency, which meant a different driver nearly every day, some of whom couldn't keep a schedule if they tried. Plus, I had to explain albinism constantly, something I hope to avoid by explaining it one last time, to you."

Pibb gave her a puzzled look. "What does being an alb — I mean, what does that have to do with my driving you about, if I may ask, madam?"

She sighed, looked down at her new bracelet, a George Jensen Möbius band given to her by Bruce, and smiled to herself.

"Good catch and good question. First off, I'm legally blind. Not blind-blind, as in seeing nothing, but poor vision to be sure."

"I would have never guessed. You seem pretty normal to me." He took a chance and waved his hands in front of him to see if she could see him.

"Oh, Mr. Pibb, please don't do that. My sight is not that bad at this distance."

"Sorry, madam, I was just, well—sorry is all." He could feel his face go red.

"No need to be embarrassed, Mr. Pibb."

"Yes, madam. So things are kind of blurry at a distance, right?"

"Not blurry exactly, Mr. Pibb. It's more like I'm looking at a low-resolution photograph with poor details."

Pibb seemed puzzled. "Sounds like blurry to me."

Luna paused. "Hmm, okay, have you ever looked through the wrong end of a telescope?"

Pibb nodded. "Yes, of course."

"It's like that. The image isn't blurred, but it somehow seems farther away."

Now Pibb was definitely confused. "I'll have to think about that a bit, madam, but can't all that be corrected with glasses?"

"Only to a certain point, but to drive I'd need a special device called a bioptic, which looks like a little telescope attached to one lens of the glasses. I tried it once, and it was just too scary for me."

"And you don't want to take cabs because of your fame."

"That, yes, although my fame, as you call it, is on the downward slope. I'll have to be considering other options soon. Perhaps my own agency. Dunno."

"Not for lack of beauty, if I may say so, madam."

Luna smiled. "Thank you, Mr. Pibb, but sadly for me, this is more and more a game for winsome waifs, not mature women." She paused and shook her head. "Anyway, a few more facts about my vision. One, my eyes look pinkish, sometimes purplish, because my irises are a very pale blue—much, much paler than yours, in fact—so what you're seeing is the blood vessels on the back of my retina."

"You don't say?"

"Two, my pupils don't dilate and contract like yours, so bright sunshine is a problem. I'll be wearing dark polarized sunglasses a lot of the time, as well as a broad-brimmed fedora like this one." She pointed to the hat on the corner of the desk, a black Borsalino she had picked up at a shoot in Florence a few years back. "Even then I will have trouble dealing with the sun and its evil twin, shade. In bright sunlight, anything in the shade goes completely dark. So if there's a mugger in the shade, I have a big problem."

"I think I know what you mean. It's like walking out of a dark movie theater into the bright sunlight. You can't see well and it's almost painful."

"That's exactly it, Mr. Pibb, except *your* eyes quickly adjust to the light and mine don't adjust at all—and it *is* painful."

"I had no idea."

"Third, my depth perception and peripheral vision are very bad."

"Oh?"

"Yes, unfamiliar stairs can be a real problem. And fourth, I know you've noticed my eyes moving back and forth. That's a condition called nystagmus—don't worry, you won't have to remember that. It's a condition that makes it difficult for me to focus on details, like that delightful mole on your chin, Mr. Pibb."

He couldn't help but reach up and touch it.

"You'll see me cock my head to find a good focal point. And the rapid eye movement will just get worse when I'm stressed or tired. You'll need to remember that. When I'm tired, I tend to take risks, sometimes foolish risks, not that that has anything at all to do with albinism. It's just me."

"I see, madam. So . . . other than all that, you see perfectly well."

Luna laughed. "Yes, Mr. Pibb, *perfectly* well."

Pibb smiled back at her, happy she seemed to appreciate his dry humor. "Well, madam, you have just defied Hoffman's Law of Hilarity."

"What?"

"A true friend will not laugh at your joke until she retells it."

"Ah, Mr. Pibb, but we're not friends. This is strictly a business arrangement, and I would expect you to comport yourself accordingly."

"Oh, of course, madam."

"One last question, Mr. Pibb. What's with all these laws you quote?"

"Well, you might say I'm a student of human behavior. And I think we're all governed by laws . . . except for those who aren't, of course."

Luna smiled. "And whose law is that, Mr. Pibb?"

Pibb shrugged. "Well, I never thought of it before, but I guess that would have to be Pibb's First Law."

"Wonderful. I can hardly wait for the second."

She grew quiet and leaned back in her chair, her hands in front of her, forming a tent.

"So, Mr. Pibb, I'll need you to be my eyes at times. Are you up for that?"

"Yes, of course."

"Then I'm happy to offer you the job." She extended her hand across the desk.

Pibb beamed and took her hand in his, surprised at her firm grip and marveling at the contrast between his skin and hers. "Thank you, madam, when do I start?"

"How about Monday morning? I already have a ride in, so meet me here at, say, 9:00 a.m. sharp? We're going to have a very full day."

"Just what I like, madam, just what I like. Um, but one thing."

"Yes?"

"We haven't talked about the car I'll be driving. Are you renting or do you already own one?"

"Ah, the limo. As it turns out, I've just purchased one from a new friend at the Saudi embassy. Haven't laid eyes on it, but my friend says it's in reasonably good condition. And I got it cheap. Anyway, he's dropping it off first thing Monday morning."

"Yes, madam, wonderful," he said, but he was thinking, *Oh, blimey, this can't be good. Probably a mechanical nightmare. I'll have to pop 'round to Jack's and have him give it a good onceover. But I have a job!*

5

Bruce's Apartment, Nottingham, October 14.

The drive home took only a few minutes, but Bruce had the distinct impression he had been followed. A black van had seemingly tailed him from the moment he left the parking lot, but then had sped off once Bruce reached his apartment.

He pulled into a parking spot, grabbed the garbage bag off the front seat, and rushed for the door, glancing in both directions to see if he could spot the van. Nothing. *I'm just being paranoid*, he thought, chiding himself. *A black van? Ridiculous. Must be watching too much TV.*

The apartment was the usual end-of-week wreck, what Luna referred to as the flotsam and jetsam of the single life: dishes piled high in the sink, empty pizza boxes and Chinese takeout cartons covering the coffee table, and the unmistakable smell of rotting food from each major food group. There was also more than a few crumpled up pieces of paper, failed pages from his overdue report. Not even working at home seemed to help, the report as scattered and rough as a gravel driveway.

He thought to deal with it all, or at least give Luna a call, but then decided he'd much rather get a fast start on the long drive to her place. He took off his business clothes, then pulled on a black Henley shirt, a pair of jeans, and his running shoes. He threw a few other things into a gym bag, along with the garbage bag, tugged on a windbreaker, took another look at the accumulated mess, shrugged, and rushed back to the car. No sign of the van. *Yes, definitely paranoid.*

6

The City Mills, Haggerston, Apartment 132.

The drive from Nottingham had been faster than he had expected, traffic on the M1 much lighter than normal, perhaps due to his early afternoon departure, but perhaps the time just seemed to pass more quickly because he was lost in thought about the package in the gym bag next to him.

Luna had not yet arrived, and perhaps wouldn't for an hour or more. The apartment was dark, as usual, when he opened the door and was greeted by the almost cloying smell of fresh flowers. Rather than switch on the lights, he hit the button near the front door that activated the automatic blinds, which rose in unison, light flooding the apartment and revealing the Hoxton-Haggerston cityscape and the distant high rises of London.

He was always startled by the apartment, particularly all the glass, which seemed an odd choice for a person with albinism, but Luna loved it for its views at night. His pet name for the apartment was "the crane" because when they had first looked at the floor plan in the agent's office, it had looked like an origami crane viewed from its side, all angles and triangles.

She had insisted on furnishing the apartment herself — it was hers after all — and he had not argued the point. They were early in their relationship then, and it wasn't clear at all how things would turn out. She had surprised him again, furnishing the apartment entirely by multiple trips to IKEA and creating in him an active dread of the words "some assembly required." It seemed a strange, frugal choice for an apartment just south of a million pounds, but Luna was like that, extravagant one minute and frugal the next, her most recent extravagance the decision to buy a limo, albeit used, and hire a chauffeur.

He quickly found the source of the smell, a large bouquet of white roses in a tall ornate vase on the dining room table, a note lying beneath it. He knew before looking at it who had sent the flowers: Ahmed Abhoud, the son of the Saudi ambassador.

The man had been a pest ever since they met him at a cocktail party just over a month ago. He had followed Luna around like a puppy, offering to freshen her drink, refill her plate with the best hors d'oeuvres, introducing her to his "very best" friends and colleagues, and generally making a jackass out of himself throughout the evening, all while trying to put himself between Luna and Bruce at every opportunity.

Bruce glanced down at the note, which was not in the least surprising: "Flowers for a flower — Ahmed." *White roses? How corny. Bastard.*

He picked up the vase and took it to the kitchen counter. She could move it back when she arrived, but for now he needed the entire table for the package. He set to work.

7

The Close Confines of Kat Murphy's 1970 Austin Mini Cooper, London, October 14.

Luna braced herself as Kat sped through the intersection, all the while looking directly at Luna and not at the road, Green Day's "American Idiot" at near full volume. One thing that she had noticed about Kat was that she tended to drive as fast as whatever music was playing on the radio.

"What on earth possessed you to buy this clown car?" said Luna at full voice, reaching over and turning down the volume from fifteen to four.

"What's not to like, honey? It's red with white racing stripes on the hood and it has those cute little tires no bigger than a medium pizza. Plus, it's fully restored. Mint."

"But just look at us, we're all elbows and knees in here. How can you *like* this?"

"Oh, hush up, honey, you know you love it."

"No, I definitely *don't* love it. Slow down, you're scaring the shit out of me."

"I'm not speeding, honey. It's just the speed thrill you get from a car this low to the ground."

"Well, slow down anyway."

Kat tapped the brakes and downshifted, the exhaust rumbling its disapproval. "Whatever."

"Anyway, as I was saying, the last interview went well, so I hired him on the spot. That means Monday morning will be my last day in the clown car."

Kat offered an exaggerated frown in mock pout. "Oh, honey, and I was just getting used to your screams."

Luna laughed but then almost screamed as Kat sped through another intersection, horns blaring all around them. "Kat, Kat, Kat!"

Kat was also a model, barely nineteen, a Georgia girl, but not really one of those winsome waifs. She was tall and blonde and built like a swimmer, with broad shoulders, long muscular legs, and narrow hips, all attributes that made her one of the darlings of *Sports Illustrated*, along with her emerald green eyes and young Charlize Theron looks.

Unlike Luna, she wore rings on several fingers and sported several earrings in each ear. Today she was wearing a short, high-necked, long-sleeved dress with white and yellow daisies on a black background, with matching, over-the-ankle yellow boots. Her small, black-fringed purse lay next to her, just behind the gear shift. She had tossed her yellow wool coat into the back seat.

Luna had taken her under her wing, helping her make her way through the gauntlet of photographers, agents, fellow models, and groupies. Kat in turn had provided transportation, when needed, to and from their apartments in the Hoxton-Haggerston area. They lived in the same building, in fact, in a complex known as The City Mills, Luna in a corner apartment on the slightly less expensive 9th floor, Kat directly above her in the penthouse on the 10th floor. Pricey digs, but they could both afford it, especially Kat, who was bringing in a ton of money, and they liked the arty feel to the community. Besides, the apartments were great investments, as their shared accountant was quick to point out.

And they were here, much to Luna's relief.

Kat pulled the car into her parking spot and turned off the engine. "Luna, have you given any thought to the Scotland gig? You know they want you on the shoot. And it would make one hell of a fun vacation. Men in kilts!"

Luna sighed. *Here we go again.* "As I told you, I'm not sure that would be a good idea. You know I have a bad history with that photographer. Besides, Bruce and I are really starting to get serious about finding a new place."

Kat screwed up her mouth and talked like a toddler. "But you need to be there to protect me from the big, bad wolf."

"Kat, you're impossible," she laughed. "Look, I'll give it some thought, okay?"

Kat beamed. "Yes! But don't wait too long to decide; the shoot starts on the 24th."

"Okay, but no promises." Luna started climbing out of the car. "Okay, then, I'll see you first thing Monday."

"Can I meet this new chauffeur?"

"Of course."

"Is he hot?"

Luna shrugged. "For a man of fifty maybe."

"Oh, *ewww*—well, maybe take a ride in the new limo? You know how much I love limos."

"We'll see."

"Okay, then. Hey, would you like to pop up for a drink later? The guy at the shop turned me on to this wonderful wine called Duct Tape Chardonnay. Their slogan is 'the wine that can fix anything.'"

Luna chuckled and shook her head. "Oh, my, sounds quite elegant and irresistible, but no, I'm expecting Bruce any minute now — if he's not hung up in traffic. A full weekend ahead."

"Lucky you. So I guess that means you won't be going to the range with me tomorrow? I want to try out my new bow."

Kat, an expert archer, had introduced the sport to Luna, even though archery seemed an unlikely sport for her. Luna had balked at first, but then Kat pointed out that the 2012 Olympic champion was a legally blind man from Korea who set a world record just by shooting at what he said was "the center of a colorful blur." Luna wasn't the most accurate archer, her accuracy going from dead-on up close to far off at any distance beyond thirty yards or so, but she thoroughly enjoyed the challenge. She didn't know how blindfolded Zen archers did it, but she would have paid good money for the knowledge.

"No, sorry."

"How about a little Parkour run tomorrow morning, then?"

Luna sighed and shook her head. Kat was an expert at Parkour, or free running, a sport that used the body's momentum to jump, climb, or overcome any obstacle, from walls to buildings. She'd taken Luna out a couple of times, but Luna was terrible at it, even though she had participated in cross country in high school. Uneven ground was one thing, but the added dimension of full-speed running at obstacles just spelled disaster for her, thanks to her poor depth perception. She had been meaning to tell Kat that she just had to quit. "Sorry again. Bruce and I will probably be, um, sleeping in."

Kat frowned. "How about breakfast on Sunday morning, then, for the three of us? If there's one thing a Georgia girl can do — and she can do many, many things — it's make breakfast. Hell, we're all about breakfast. You have *got* to taste my biscuits."

Luna was already shaking her head.

"Well, shit then," Kat said, disappointed. "Ya'll have a good one, I guess. Fuck yourselves silly."

They both slammed their doors shut and walked into the building, Luna saying goodbye as she stepped off the elevator on the ninth floor, Kat waving silently, still pouting.

8

The City Mills, Haggerston, Apartment 132.

When Luna opened the door, she was pleasantly surprised to see Bruce already there, sitting at the dining room table, poring over what appeared to be hand-written documents, a small book, and a pile of strange shell fragments.

Every Friday was like meeting him for the first time all over again. She loved his broad-shouldered, rugged looks. No pretty boy, for sure, but still handsome, sexy even, with long sandy-blond hair, ice blue eyes, and a nose and jaw that looked like they had been sculpted by Michelangelo. He was just the right height. When they embraced, everything just seemed to fit: arms here, hips there, lips and eyes locked. *We're like Legos*, she thought.

"Cheers," she said brightly, doffing her fedora and placing it on a small table near the door, along with her purse and sunglasses. As she slipped out of her jacket and draped it on a chair, she glanced out the windows at the already twinkling skyline, a city coming to life for a long Friday night.

Bruce waved hello but kept his eyes on his find. "Luna, you will not *believe* what I've found."

She came over, leaned in, and gave him a long kiss. "Well, I hope it's your appetite — I'm starving."

He beamed up at her. "Far better. I've found nothing less than two previously unknown letters of Charles Darwin, along with a new journal chronicling an incredible encounter he had with a man in Tierra del Fuego who claimed to be 431 years old."

Luna couldn't help laughing. "What? That's crazy."

Bruce shook his head emphatically. "Well, that's not the half of the craziness, but they seem to be genuine. The paper, the ink, his handwriting. It all seems genuine, or at least I think it is."

Luna was incredulous. "And you would know this how?"

"I wrote a paper in grad school about Darwin. I've seen some of his original letters, and this — this — looks spot on."

Luna sighed and shook her head. "Oh, Bruce, how could you *possibly* accept *any* of this? Darling, we're talking about staid old Darwin, the old man in the beard, a scientist through and through. You're dreaming if you think this is real. I mean, come on, a man how old?"

"431 years."

She raised her pale eyebrows. "Seriously?"

"Okay, I know it sounds silly. But look, the man *claimed* to be that old. Darwin didn't believe it for a minute. And we're not talking about Darwin, the old man in the beard. This is Darwin on the *Beagle* voyage, when he was just 25 years old, or nearly, and making discovery after discovery."

Luna sat down next to him and glanced at the documents and the shell fragments. "Okay, let's both be crazy and say you're right. What's with the shells?"

"Well, if the documents and journal are to be believed, they are the fragments of a dragon egg."

She clapped her hands together. "What? Oh, this just gets better and better, nothing farfetched here."

"I *said* there was more craziness."

Luna held up both hands, palms out. "Okay, now, just wait. Please start at the beginning. Where did you get this stuff?"

Bruce smiled at her. "The most amazing thing. Old Nozzle had me clean out an old storage area we call the gloomy corner, and there they were, under a pile of boxes, inside a broken-open barrel. A small cask, really."

Luna rolled her eyes. "I wish you wouldn't call him that. He has a name."

"Yes, but he also has that nose."

Luna sighed. "Okay, again, let's say all this—all this *craziness*—is real, and of course it's *not*. What next?"

Bruce shrugged. "That's my quandary at the moment. Do I turn them over to Old—I mean, to Dr. Shepherd—on Monday morning, or do I take the time to authenticate them?"

"Either way, you're going to have to deal with the fact that Shepherd will be upset that you even *thought* to take this stuff home."

Bruce nodded. "Yes, that's a given."

"So I'd say authenticate them if you can. I mean, the whole 431-year-old man thing could be embarrassing to say the least, not to mention the so-called dragon egg."

"Indeed."

And then something dawned on her. "Wait, wait, wait—do you think someone is setting you up?"

Bruce hadn't considered that, but now it seemed to make some sense, and he knew just the person. "You mean someone like Jamie?"

"The very one," said Luna, nodding. "He had access, and he certainly hates your guts. This would certainly be the perfect way to get rid of you. At least make you out to be a fool."

He thought back to their encounter earlier in the day. *Why did Jamie just show up there? Did he want to make sure I found what he had planted? Then again, Old Nozzle had said Jamie was against cleaning out the gloomy corner. Or was his objection just a ruse?* "It's possible, it's *definitely* possible."

"Then I think we have your answer. Unless you just throw all of this away—I mean, you know you're being punked, right?—you'll need an expert who can debunk the whole thing, so you can turn this back on Jamie. Question is do you know who could authenticate this stuff, and by *authenticate* I mean show it to be a hoax?"

Bruce didn't have to think long. "Professor Wilson at Queen Mary's. You remember, we met him at that cocktail party last month. When he learned that I was with the Survey, he just went on and on about Darwin."

Luna shook her head. "Nope."

"The one with the beard."

"Bruce, *most* of your friends have beards."

"Point taken," he said. "You'll remember him when you see him."

"Okay, sounds like a plan. Now, two things. Do you mind if I have a look at these and would you please put a pizza in the oven—my stomach is about to turn inside out."

"No and yes," he said, heading for the kitchen. "I thought you would, so I made enlarged copies for you."

"Thank you. You are such a sweetie."

"And while you're reading, I'll see if I can track down Professor Wilson. I think we exchanged cards. May have it in my wallet." He pulled open the freezer drawer and pulled out two pizzas. "Pepperoni or Everything?"

Luna didn't hesitate. "I am totally in the mood for everything right about now, and the faster the better." She turned back to the documents and began to read. *This is just silly.*

9

The City Mills, Haggerston, Apartment 132.

Luna picked up a copy of one of the letters, which was addressed to a Reverend Professor John Stevens Henslow, Cambridge, and dated 12 February 1834. She began to read, stopping from time to time to parse out his difficult handwriting.

My Dear Henslow

If you are reading this, I am either quite dead or, alternatively, standing next to you, bursting with excitement.—If neither, than surely I am in Bedlam, for my story alone. In any case, it is time to explain the events & discoveries of 6-7 February 1834, & decide what should be done with the enclosed journal, egg, & barnacles. Particularly the barnacles, some of which are unlike anything I have ever seen before, & worthy of extensive study alone. I pray you followed my instructions & secreted away this small cask, so that its contents remained safe & secure in my absence. — You will also note that I have included a similar letter to my sisters in the event you decide to share the journal with them after my death. I wanted to put their minds at ease that I was not—am not—void of my senses, although upon reading my journal, I can certainly appreciate how anyone might think otherwise & send me Bedlam bound. — Given these discoveries, I cannot decide whether to continue on this voyage or find speedy transport home. — I am in a quandary, but you now know which decision I have taken. — I put all my trust & faith in you, as I have done these many years.

Till then believe me, my dear Henslow; Yours very truly obliged,

Chas Darwin. —

Please break this news gently to my sisters, if circumstances so warrant.

Luna put off reading the letter to Darwin's sisters for now, knowing it would probably be much the same as the letter to Henslow. She wanted to get to the meat of it. *Meat.* The smell of the baking pizza made her stomach growl, and she could hear Bruce talking excitedly on his cell phone, apparently to this Professor Wilson. She turned to the copy of the journal and began reading.

February 6. Upon hearing a fantastical story about the death of the previous captain, Pringle Stokes, & a creature half man & half dragon, I asked & was granted permission by FitzRoy to go ashore in search of what I thought & hoped would be an as yet uncatalogued bird, monsters to my mind being mundane things observed incorrectly. — If only that had been the case, for there was no great white bird, which I will get to presently.

We had taken safe harbour in Port Famine, under the looming presence of Mount Tarn, three days previously, but until today, the weather kept us on board. —To make the most of the day, we started just before dawn, we being myself, my steadfast assistant, Syms Covington, & two seamen, Rowlett & Martens, whom FitzRoy had demanded I take along, on the off chance that we could return with some guanaco meat for the crew.

Traveling this desolate lanscape in cold gale winds was arduous, & none of us expected to make it to the higest peak.— Yet we pushed on as best we could until a guanaco bounded out of a deep ravine and ran right by us, the other three giving chase & firing as best they could.

& then I was alone. From the ever fainter sound of their voices, I knew it would be a long while before they returned, so I decided to press on for as far & as high as I could.— My efforts were soon rewarded by an amazing sight: smoke rising from the mouth of a cave.

Not wanting to surprise whomever was camped there, I shouted out to announce myself.— But I was greeted by silence.— I called again & still nothing.

I approached the opening & peered into the darkness. A small young man with alabaster skin, a man unlike any Fuegian, sat in front of a small fire, staring out at me.— He said nothing at first, but beckoned me into the cave with a wave of his hand, which I could see had fingernails grown to an almost impossible length, the unevenness of their growth causing them to coil like the ringlets of my dear sister Susan's hair.

He looked peacible, so I stooped and shuffled in as best I could, the roof of the cave being quite low at the entrance but opening to a large cavern once inside.— He motioned me to sit, which I did, letting my eyes grow accustomed to the light, which was dim despite the fire.

I could see clearly now that he was a Chinaman, & judging from his almost red eyes & long white-blonde hair & beard, one afflicted with that condition that makes a man near devoid of colour in every way.

He was dressed head to toe in guanaco skins, but not after the lose fashion of the Fuegian savages & their seal skin capes.— His clothing appeared to have been made by a fine tailor, one who might do good business in London. He cleared his throat, as if he had not spoken a word in days, & smiled at me.

"You are from the ship." The words came out haltingly at first but flowed more freely once he had become accustomed to speaking English, which was clearly not his primary language. "Has my friend Captain Stokes had a change of heart after so many years?"

His words startled me to the core, & it took a few moments for me to collect myself.

"Is something the matter?" he said.

"No—I mean yes. Mr. Stokes is dead. Shot himself some years ago, right in this harbour."

The man seemed visibly shaken. "I did not know this, and it saddens me to hear it." He shook his head. "But he was a nervous man, & I fear I have had a part in his death."

He reached across the fire and offered me his hand. "I am Zhao Yu," he said, "Guardian of the White Dragon on the sixth voyage of the treasure fleet, & humble servant of Emperor Zhu Di, may he forever reign in life and memory."

Luna sat back in her chair. "Holy shit!"

Bruce sensed where she was in the journal. "Zhao Yu?"

"Yes, what the fuck!"

"Keep reading, there's more."

"When will that damned pizza be ready? The smell is intoxicating."

Bruce snorted. "I'm surprised you can smell *anything* other than these damn roses."

Luna looked up. Bruce had shoved the vase of roses flat up against the side of the refrigerator in what looked to be a less than friendly way. "We're not jealous are we?"

"No, and of course I am."

"Oh, Bruce, he means nothing, the roses mean nothing, but he is a nice man."

"So you say."

"He's given me a great deal on a limo."

"Sight unseen."

"I trust him, and he's being very sweet. Besides, if the limo's a lemon, I'll insist that he refund my money. Now, what's the timing on that damn pizza?"

"Still five minutes or so. Finish up if you can, and we'll talk — and eat."

She returned to the journal.

I haltingly introduced myself as the natural philosopher of the Beagle, & overcome by curiosity, asked whether he was known to the Fuegians as "the pale man of the mountain," which prompted a hearty laugh from him.

He explained that the term referred to his son, who was born with the gift of flight. In that moment, I knew that I was dealing with a man quite out of his senses, & looked for every opportunity to make my excuses & depart. — But despite myself, I was transfixed by this man & the story he told me.

He said that his son, Zhao Jiao-long, had indeed flown to the Beagle to implore Stokes to grant him passage to England, as he had done day after day during the previous weeks, only to find Stokes holed up in his cabin. "My son has a terrible temper, & no doubt grew impatient enough to threaten poor Captain Stokes."

At this point, I told him the stories recounted by Mr. May, of a creature that looked at once like a man and a dragon, & the man was not surprised. "He looks like a dragon, because he is half man & half dragon."

I started to ask another question, but he asked me to listen instead to his full story before making assumptions or asking questions. — So I sat in silence as he proceeded to unfold his fantastical story, which has led me to believe now that the insane make for the best liars.

His story, he claimed, began in China, in our year 1421. — He had been chosen & trained from birth, he said, to be the guardian of one of the Emperor's dragons. — People like him, whom he called "the pale," were said to have magical powers, one of which was a calming effect on dragons.

Whatever powers he might have had, they were not enough to stem a plague that was sweeping through the ranks of the Emperor's dragons, which had numbered in the hundreds, but now had been reduced to his most powerful dragon, a red dragon of immense size & power that seemed unaffected by the plague, & the eggs of four other dragons, each laid just prior to their mothers' death.

Seeking safety for these eggs, the Emperor decided in secret to ship them to the four corners of the world, so that they might hatch & thrive & one day return. To make sure of their safety, he appointed four pale guardians to accompany them on the voyage.

Zhao Yu, then twenty-one, had been granted the great honor to be entrusted with the egg of the last white dragon. — Three other pale were entrusted with the eggs of three other dragons, each assigned to the flagships of the four admirals selected to make the sixth voyage of the treasure fleet. — Each admiral knew the destination for their dragon egg, but not for the others. — The rest of the seamen, apart from the guardians, knew nothing.

At that time, it seems, the empire was under assault from all directions, & the Emperor knew that without his dragons, he would be challenged. — It was long believed that the Red Dragon could only be defeated by a dragon that had devoured the bodies of at least three other dragons, incorporating the powers of the other dragons & growing ever more powerful as it fed.

So it was that the destinations of the eggs were held in highest secrecy, lest the Emperor's enemies find the eggs & create a dragon capable of defeating the Red Dragon.

At this point I thought to interrupt his story to ask why the Emperor had not just destroyed the eggs and thus prevented any challenge, but I decided to honour his request & let him finish his story.

So at the start of the voyage, each egg was placed securely in a net & placed below the water line of each admiral's junk. — The guardians would check the eggs throughout the day to assure their safety.

"Pizza!" Bruce shouted from the kitchen.

She set down the journal pages and walked to the counter, where Bruce had arranged plates, served up the pizza, and poured two glasses of beer.

"You are my hero," she said, taking a big bite of pizza. "Just what I need."

"So did you finish day one?"

"No, still a little more, but I must say I'm a bit blown away by how elaborate this hoax is." She took another big bite.

"Still think it's a hoax, eh?"

"Of course, don't you? I mean, if you're going to the trouble of setting up this hoax, why so many misspelled words? And the actions of this so-called emperor seem illogical. Why preserve the eggs at all? And why does Zhao Yu know so much when the mission was supposed to be so secret?"

"Well, keep reading. Darwin—or Hoax Darwin, if you will—has some answers for you." He took a sip of beer. "Oh, I was able to reach Professor Wilson. He'll see us tomorrow morning at nine in his university office."

Luna seemed crestfallen. "Must we? What about our house hunting plans? I was so looking forward to it."

Bruce sat down his glass. "I suppose I could call him back and try to reschedule, but I'd really like to get some answers before I have to face Shepherd and confront Jamie on Monday."

Luna held up her hand. "Stop, perhaps we can do both. If this Wilson is the expert you claim he is, he should be able to tell us straight off if we're looking at Darwin's handwriting or not."

"Okay, great." He finished his beer in one gulp, stood, and pushed his stool back under the counter. "If you don't mind, I think I'll jump in the shower. Give you some time to finish reading."

"I think that would be an excellent idea, sir," she said holding her nose. "You are a tad rank."

Bruce chuckled. "I blame it on the gloomy corner."

"But wait, you've only had one slice."

"Not that hungry, actually."

She looked down at the pizza. There were still three pieces left. "Well, don't expect to find any pizza when you return. I'm famished."

"Oh, how I wish I had a metabolism like yours," he said.

"Jealous, are we? Well, off you go. I have to finish with Mr. Darwin."

He gave her a kiss on the cheek, grabbed his gym bag, and headed for the bathroom. "You could join me, you know."

She laughed and wagged a finger at him. "No, thank you, sir. I don't shower with men who stink. Besides, I'm a dedicated reader. You dare not distract me. Perhaps another time."

Ten minutes later, three additional slices of pizza resting comfortably in her stomach, all held firmly in place by her six-pack abs, the product of strict physical training, including free weights, a martial art known as Wing Chun, and running. She returned to the dining room table and picked up the journal.

Life aboard ship was anything but pleasurable for Zhao Yu, some of the crew treating him as if he were stupid, an apparently common misperception about the pale, while others thought he was bad luck, openly harassing him. — So by the time they reached the Cape of Good Hope, where the four fleets parted, Zhao Yu had isolated himself as much as possible from the crew, taking his meals alone & only appearing on deck when it was time to check on the egg cradled safely in the net.

As he checked the egg each day, he began to notice barnacles appearing on its surface. He was reluctant to scrape them off, he said, for fear that his actions might crack the egg & kill the dragon growing inside.

By the time they had crossed the Atlantic & arrived at the tip of South America, the egg was fully encrusted with barnacles. — Now Zhao Yu worried whether the little dragon would have the strength to break out.

As they sailed through the Straights of Magellan—my God, nearly a century before Magellan's "discovery"—a terrible storm blew up, sinking seven of the junks, including his.

"Just before it sank, I managed to cut loose the net & dive into the sea. Seventeen of us made it to shore. I'm sorry to say, sixteen of us thought I was the bad luck that had brought on the storm. So as they set up camp on shore, I fled up the mountain with the egg. & I have been here since."

& then Zhao Yu stopped.

"I can see so many questions growing in your eyes," he said. "Best stop now."

Luna looked up as Bruce came back into the room. He was wearing red tartan pajama bottoms and a white tee-shirt.

"Still reading, I see," he said, rubbing a towel across his head.

"Yes, not as fast as you, I'm afraid. His handwriting is atrocious, and this is all hard on my eyes, even with the enlargement."

"You can stop, you know."

"No, no, it's still pretty fascinating stuff—for a *hoax*."

"All right, keep at it. I'm going to make another copy to leave behind with Professor Wilson. He may not be as quick to judge as we think."

"All right." She flipped ahead through the remaining pages. "This shouldn't take too long."

"Do you still have that magnifying glass? I'd like to take a closer look at the shell fragments."

"With these eyes? Yes, of course, first drawer on the right."

She turned back to the journal.

I implored him to continue, but he said he had grown tired. — He asked me to return tomorrow, with some tea and a sack. —I had no problem bringing tea, but I was curious about the sack. When I asked him why I should bring a sack, he said, "That is yet another question, & it reminds me of a folk tale told to me by my master when I was very young."

He then went on to relate the story of a young man named Wei, who despite his labours could not get rich. — Wei decided the only way to get what he wanted was to visit a wise man at the top of Holy Mountain & ask him how to get rich. Along the way, he met a woman who imploured him to ask the wise man why her daughter never smiled. — The next day he came upon a town, where everyone was sad because their magnolia tree had stopped blossoming. They wanted Wei to ask the wise man how to make it bloom again. — Wei traveled on and came upon a river with a fierce current that made it impassable. As he sat crestfallen on its bank, a dragon approached, granting him passage across the river if he would agree to ask the wise man why he could no longer fly like other dragons.

Finally Wei climbed to the top of the mountain. "I have four questions," he said to the wise man, who laughed at him & said, "I will but grant you three questions." Wei thought to ask his question first, but because of the kindnesses shown him along his journey, he asked the other questions.

"How can the dragon fly again?" The wise man never hesitated. "Dragons are known for hoarding jewels; your dragon must toss them aside; then & only then, thus freed from their weight, will he be able to fly again."

"Why does the magnolia tree fail to bloom?" The wise man tilted his head slyly. "The tree is hindered by a chest of gold entangled in its roots. The villagers must dig up the gold, & the tree will blossom once more."

"How can a mother make her daughter smile?" The wise man chuckled. "Oh, that's the easiest of all. She will smile when she sees the man she will love & live with for the rest of her days."

& so it was that Wei's question went unanswered. — He made his way back down the mountain to the rushing river, where he gave the dragon his answer. The dragon was so delighted, he handed a sack of jewels to Wei & flew away.

Wei walked on, back to the village & the magnolia tree. When he told them their answer, they immediately set to digging. Once the chest of gold was uncovered the tree blossomed in all its glory. So pleased were the villagers that they gave the gold to Wei as a reward for his efforts on their behalf.

Wei arrived the next day at the house of the woman, but when he knocked on her door, the daughter appeared instead & immediately smiled at him. He was overcome with love & spent the rest of his days with her in peace & prosperity.

"Tale has many meanings," Zhao Yu said. "One is that it is better to be selfless than selfish, to take care of the dragon's needs before your own, but in your case, Mr. Darwin, the lesson is to ask the right questions. Bring your right questions to me tomorrow, & I will have answers & a gift for you."

I have been thinking of nothing else since I left the cave.

Luna set down the journal pages, which caught Bruce's eye. He had come back into the room after briefly examining the shell fragments — the magnifying glass hadn't helped all that much — and had been anxiously waiting for her to finish, so they could at least discuss the text, but he knew she couldn't possibly be through.

"Why are you stopping?" he said.

Luna looked over at him. "I'm at the end of the first day."

"Ah, the folk tale."

"Yes, and I was wondering what questions I would ask, especially if I were held to just three."

"We can discuss that now if you like, but it would be better to press on to day two, where you'll get the answers, or at least some of them."

Luna shook her head. "You know what, I'm really tired. I'm going to call it a day and pick this up again in the morning. I never thought interviewing people could be so draining, but I'm just . . . *pooped*."

Bruce looked disappointed, but she was having none of it.

"Don't give me that look. I really wouldn't be a good partner at the moment. Besides, you know I get up early. I'll read the rest before you even wake up, and we can discuss it all at breakfast. I'll even make banana pancakes."

"Well, I'd much prefer sex to pancakes, but . . . deal," said Bruce. "And speaking of eating, you've done it again."

"What?"

"Your blouse."

Luna looked down. Three globs of pizza sauce decorated her blouse, accented by a large coffee stain, apparently from earlier in the day. "Oh, shit, not again." *Had Mr. Pibb seen the coffee stain? Oh, crap.*

Bruce shook his head and laughed. "I can't take you anywhere."

Luna walked to the kitchen to get a wet cloth to deal with the stains. "You got that right."

10

The Tip and Diddle Pub, London, October 14.

Pontius Pibb was in the mood for a little celebration, so before heading home, where no one but his cat, Lucifer, was waiting, he stopped in to his favorite pub for a pint or three. More likely, just a pint, and perhaps a snack if he had enough money, which was unlikely, the toll of not having a job steadily reducing his funds to near nil.

He didn't know how old the Tip and Diddle was, but it was friendly enough — no damned tourists for one — and dim enough for a man to lose himself in a sea of wood paneling and polished brass without feeling the need to talk up a single soul.

That was his plan — a quiet evening in a dark corner with a dark, warm beer — but life was about to invoke a law familiar to Pibb, and he wondered whether to say it out loud: *Pangraze's Law of Planning, namely, to assure success, plan backward from whatever result you get.*

Instead, he just said, "Hello, Jack, good to see you."

Another good thing about the Tip and Diddle was that no one, not even the proprietor, cared to invoke a dress code of any kind. So a man in a prim chauffer's uniform sat opposite a man in the greasy uniform of a mechanic who'd had his fair share of spurting oil and petrol for one day. And that was just fine. They could have been in tuxedos or completely naked. It just didn't matter here.

Pibb glanced over at Jack Barney. He could never decide whether the man used motor oil on his hair or some fancy goop, but his hair was swept back over his head in a way that suggested he was wearing a shiny black helmet. He was a powerfully built man, with hands as big as paddles and legs as thick as trees, but if you were asked to describe him, the first thing you'd mention would be his gleaming gold tooth. That, or his eyes, which were gray as winter and set wide above a nose flattened and twisted by too many fights, in and outside the ring. You did not want to mess with this man, because you would be seeing stars before you hit the floor.

Pibb did mess with him, though, in two fights back in the nineties — Jack "The Mauler" Barney vs. Pontius "The Pilot" Pibb — both draws, one fight giving Jack the opportunity for his gold tooth, the other giving Pibb a jaw that now ached every time it rained. Through respect and shared pain, they had become fast friends.

"My, you're all dressed up. Whatever for?" said Jack, turning to give the proprietor a quick nod, which was received with a wink and a quick move for a glass. The man knew him well and knew to be quick about his business.

"Interview for a job. Had to spruce up a bit, a'course."

"Any luck then?" The proprietor set a pint in front of him without a word, and retreated to the bar.

Pibb raised his glass. "Indeed, I am now the chauffeur to none other than a supermodel extraordinaire, one Moon Indigo."

Jack looked pleased and then puzzled. "Good for you! Um, I don't think I know her."

"Well, if you saw her, you'd remember. She's very pale, has albinism."

"Of course, yes, I saw her picture somewhere or other last week, some sort of perfume ad. White Tiger or White Lily or something. She's a stunner, isn't she?"

Pibb nodded and winked. "She is indeed. But say, let me ask you something."

"Sure, what's up?"

"When I asked her what I'd be driving, she says a secondhand limo from the Saudi embassy."

"So?"

"Well, I know you handle repairs for a lot of limos. I was just curious if you happened to do work for the Saudis."

Jack shook his head. "No, those blokes, most embassies in fact, handle that themselves. Security and all. I deal strictly with the commercial trade, party limos and such. More used condoms than repairs most of the time."

Pibb took another sip of beer and wiped his lips. "Pity. I was hoping you'd know something. The thing is, she's gone and bought the limo sight unseen. I'm worried it may be a little left of center."

Jack tilted his head from side to side, considering the possibilities. "It could go either way. Might be a gem. What surprises me, though, is that they're selling one of their limos to an outsider. Never heard of that. I suppose it's possible, but never heard of it."

"Is that so? Well, anyway, Jack, any chance you could take a look at her, give her a thorough look-see. I don't want to break down."

Jack nodded enthusiastically. "Oh, I would *love* that, Ponty. Bring her 'round, and I'll have a look. No charge. I've always been curious about the armor on those battleships."

"Armor?"

"Yes, indeed. Armor, bulletproof glass, communication upgrades, you name it. Those limos are loaded. This will be fun!"

Pibb raised his glass in a quiet toast, and clinked Jack's glass. "Sounds like, Jack. Say, are you hungry? I feel like ignoring Carlson's Law."

Jack shook his head. "Dammit, Ponty, you and your rules. What's it this time?"

"Don't ever try to eat where they don't want to feed you."

The proprietor glared at him. "I heard that, you know."

11

The City Mills, Haggerston, Apartment 132, October 15, 2016, Morning.

Luna wondered whether she'd ever get used to having Bruce in her bed all night. He was a thrasher, and she was a light sleeper and used to having the bed to herself, the perfect recipe for a near sleepless night. So her plan to exercise or take a short run through the park was abandoned.

She threw back the duvet and padded to the bathroom for her morning three: pee, brush, and shower. When she came back into the bedroom, Bruce was still asleep, snoring softly. *At least he's a decent snorer.*

She pulled open the chest of drawers, pulled out panties and a bra, and walked back into the bathroom to deal with her hair. The new do was still a shock and had caused quite a stir at the agency. Still, short hair was much easier to deal with, except of course for bed head. Even this punk style was problematic.

Finally satisfied, she went back to the bedroom, where she completed her wardrobe with old jeans, a long-sleeved tee shirt, and running shoes. She also pulled out a light jacket, one with a hood, just in case it rained, which it probably would judging from the gray clouds scudding along the skyline. As she left the bedroom, she remembered her new bracelet and doubled back to snatch it off the dresser.

When she walked into the kitchen, she was nearly overcome from the smell of the now somewhat wilted roses. She grabbed the flowers and threw them in the trash, placing the vase in the sink to deal with later. *Will Bruce notice?*

Banana pancakes. She wanted to start reading, but thought to at least assemble the ingredients, so she could prepare the pancakes quickly and dash. She couldn't wait to hear what this Professor Wilson would have to say, even though she expected him to laugh in their faces. *Preposterous,* he would say. *Preposterous!*

She put the dry ingredients in a bowl, set an egg and a "dead" banana, black and mushy, beside it, and made sure the milk was handy, along with a whisk, a ladle, a spatula, and a cast iron griddle. Now she could devote herself to the journal once again. She sat down at the dining room table and picked up where she'd left off.

February 8. Yesterday's events so drained me that I have not been able to return to this journal until this morning. — Yesterday, the four of us returned once again to Mount Tarn, despite a cold drizzle & biting winds. I had brought along some tea, the finest I have, as a gift for Zhao Yu, as well as a small sack for whatever gift he had a mind to give me. — I also brought a gun, thinking — rightly as it turned out—that it would be best to kill a guanaco before even climbing to the heights of Mount Tarn.

Not thirty minutes into our climb, we came upon several guanacos, & were able to quickly dispatch two. — I then directed the others to take our kills back to the ship, saying that FitzRoy was insistent that the meat be returned quickly, so that the men could enjoy a good meal for a change.— They readily complied, thinking themselves fortunate to be out of the weather, and after giving my gun to Covington, I resumed my steady climb to the cave.

The climb was treacherous & much slower than my previous climb, thanks to the dismal rain, which mirrored every surface, but I arrived without harm to myself, which is always a good thing when climbing in this unforgiving lanscape.

Zhao Yu greeted me at the opening of the cave, the first & only time that I would see him standing.— He was short, barely above five feet tall by my estimation, & as ghostly thin as he was ghostly white, the guanaco skins providing not much in the way of bulk.— How could a man this slight in nature be entrusted with a dragon? Dragons! I kept asking myself why I had even bothered to come back to talk to this man, a man clearly out of his senses.— Still, as you well know, Henslow, Nature will tell you a direct lie if she can. I can't count the number of times on this voyage alone I have found a species unlike any other. Why discount even a dragon out of hand? Perhaps what he calls a dragon is just another species of reptile as yet undiscovered in our modern world. & what a find that would be! & what if he refers to some bird as his son, & not some half man, half dragon!— Alas, there was no large white bird to be had, for his story grew stranger still.

He beckoned me into the cave without a word, & I readily complied, so eager was I to ask my questions & receive answers. But that was not to be for some time, Yu insisting that we first have tea, in a ceremony (or so he called it) involving various crudely fashioned teapots, bowls, & cups that he had fashioned out of shells and poorly fired clay, the whole process made painfully slow because of the length of the nails on his left hand. Everything had to be done with his right hand. — It was as maddening as waiting for FitzRoy to enter into a conversation.

He had a curious way of brewing the tea, rejecting the first brew after just a few seconds & pouring it into a special bowl for this purpose, so as to "release the gods" in the tea, he said. — The second brew could not have been more than fifteen seconds, but this he served, & I must admit, it was better & more fulsome than any that I had tasted previously aboard ship.

Finally setting aside our cups, again in a way that appeared to have been long practised, he settled in beside the fire, prompting it back to life with a small branch from a beech tree. — He said but a single word, "so," motioning with his hands that I could now speak. I didn't hesitate.

"So," I said, "I have several questions, the first being how you know so much about your Emperor's secret mission, when he apparently took great care to hide its scope from even his revered admirals."

Yu smiled. "The pale are thought to have little or no intelligence. As incorrect as that is, it offered us a bit of safety. By pretending to be so, we were as good as invisible in the Emperor's view, & certainly no threat to him or the empire. So rather than telling us separately our own small part in the plan, he called all four of us together & described the plan very slowly, in great detail, & then again to make sure we understood. It was agonizing & demeaning, but we all acted the part."

"So the other three guardians know everything as well?"

He nodded & beckoned me to continue.

I then asked why the Emperor chose to send the eggs to sea rather than just smashing them instead, thus ending any threat then and there.

"The answer is both easy and complication," he said. "Easy answer is to destroy the eggs would have set even his closest friends & allies against him, as well as his enemies. To do so would have been an affront to Nature. To destroy even one dragon would be unthinkable."

"Then why," I asked, "would his enemies think to have one dragon consume the three others?"

Yu frowned. "Here is beginning of complication. You see, if one dragon consumes another, the essence of the consumed dragon is not lost, but made manifest in the other."

He could tell I was having trouble with his explanation, so he continued on for some minutes describing what he called the five elements, which he said represented the "natural movements" of life.— Each of the five dragons represented one of the elements. The red dragon represented fire; the yellow dragon, earth; the blue dragon, water; the green dragon, wood; & the white dragon, metal.

Each dragon also represented a season & a direction: the red dragon, summer & south; the blue dragon, winter & north; the green dragon, spring & east; the white dragon, autumn & west; & finally, the yellow dragon, representing late summer & the center.

As you well know, Henslow, I am not a man who believes in superstition, so I did not press Yu for any further explanation.— What people do in the name of their beliefs is simply what they do, whether for good or ill.

But Yu would not let me drop the subject quite yet.—
He went on to explain that the Emperor thus sent each of
the dragons to a location that best suited them—the blue
dragon to the north, the green dragon to the east, the
yellow dragon to the center, midway between the other
locations, & the white dragon to the west.

"The problem is," said Yu, "my egg, the white dragon,
never made it to whatever west was intended, so if
someone were to find the other dragons, it is unlikely
that they would find me, although—"

"Or the white dragon," I said, interrupting him.

He gave me the strangest look & then closed his eyes
for some seconds before resuming. "No," he said, "the
white dragon is dead."

"Ha!" said Luna. "Of course, because there *is* no white
dragon."

She dropped the pages on the table and went to the wall
switch that controls the blinds. It was still dark, but she knew the
rising sun would be giving her fits, so she flipped the switch and
watched the blinds slowly close down on her view of the world.

She settled in again at the dining room table. "Come on,
Darwin boy, let's get to the other questions."

Although I was not expecting a dragon of any kind,
dead or alive, I was startled by his statement & sought to
inquire about the manner of its death.— Yu waved that
question off.

"First," he said, "important thing about dragons.
Enemies would never be able to find the dragons, unless
by luck. But dragons? Dragons can sense the presence of

other dragons across great distances. As dragons hatch, they will seek out each other and fight for power."

"But since your dragon is dead, you're safe."

Yu slowly shook his head. "Dragon dead, yes, but not my sons. Other dragons would be aware of them & seek them out wherever they are."

"Sons?" I said. "I don't understand. I thought you had just the one."

"Two sons. Zhao Jiao-long and Zhao Ju-long. One born, one not."

I told him I didn't understand, whereupon our conversation took a surprising turn. "Your other questions are how could I possibly be so old, how could there be creatures half man & half dragon, & where are these creatures? Obviously, if such creatures exist—& they do— I would fully expect you to demand to see them. & maybe you wonder what happened to the sixteen men who forced me up the mountainside." Those and more.

Bruce's voice startled her.

"Morning!" He was already dressed and ready to go. Another pair of jeans, another black Henley shirt. *Typical.*

"Well, you're pretty chipper for a man who thrashed around all night."

He glanced over at the kitchen counter, where he could see the ingredients ready for action. He could also see that the white roses were gone. *Good.*

"So, are we going to have banana pancakes, or what? We need to get started if we're going to make it to that appointment."

"I haven't finished reading."

"Where are you?"

"Zhao Yu is about to explain how he could be so old, and stuff."

"Ah. Okay, here's the plan. You prepare the pancakes while I gather the documents and shell fragments we'll need for the meeting, and I'll explain the rest of the journal to you on the way. Deal?"

Luna nodded. "Perfect. My eyes were already getting tired. It's so — so — complicated, and weird."

She stood and started toward the kitchen, and Bruce burst out laughing.

"What?"

"Your tee shirt."

She had completely forgotten she'd tugged on a tee shirt for the band Imagine Dragons, a group whose concert they had attended just a few months before. She absolutely loved them. Bruce, not so much. "Just thought I'd get in the spirit of today's business, is all."

"Well done — you rock!"

"Okay, enough," she said, pushing by him. "There's griddling to do."

She walked into the kitchen. Time to do her magic with a black banana.

12

The Vast Expanses of Bruce Cargo's 1996 Range Rover, London, October 15.

Luna greatly preferred Bruce's car over Kat's clown car. She liked sitting higher up, with more knee and elbow room, and felt protected by the sheer bulk of the vehicle, even though she could have done without the smell of mildew that came with this old car. The pine scent deodorizer swaying from the mirror just wasn't doing the trick.

"So," she said, "which campus again?"

Bruce glanced over briefly. "Queen Mary, the Arts 2 building, room 2.30 or some such. It's on the card." He took a business card out of his pocket and handed it to Luna.

"Professor Simon F. Wilson, Professor of the History of Science and Medicine," she read. "Sounds good, and yes, room 2.30."

And then she started to giggle.

"What's with you?" Bruce said. "You're absolutely pixilated."

"I was just thinking, all this talk of questions reminds me of that scene in *Monty Python and the Holy Grail*, when they're trying to get across the bridge and they have to answer three questions or be launched into the abyss."

Bruce chimed in, changing his voice to mimic the bridge keeper. "And the bridge keeper says, 'Answer me these questions three, 'ere the other side you see.'"

Luna giggled and lowered her voice. "What is your name?"

"It is Arthur, King of the Britains."

"What is your quest?"

"To seek the Holy Grail."

"What is the airspeed velocity of an unladen swallow?"

"What? African or European?"

"What? I don't know that!"

Bruce laughed. "And into the abyss the bridge keeper goes."

"Oh, my god, what a *great* movie."

Bruce downshifted and slowed the car to a stop at an intersection. "Okay, then, we're already halfway there. Won't be long now." The light changed and he made yet another turn on the zigzag route from Haggerston to Queen Mary. "At least it's Saturday. I bet this would be miserable on a weekday."

"Indeed," she said. "Okay, then, to the serious questions. What happened next in the journal?"

"Let's see now, right, one of the questions was how he could possibly be so old."

"Impossibly old."

"Yes, well, if his answer is to be believed, just before they set sail with the dragon egg, he was given a transfusion of blood from the red dragon, which assured his near immortality."

"Near?"

"Yes, it seems he can live forever, free of diseases and aging and such, but he can still be killed. Gun, knife, whatever. No silver bullets or such."

"Interesting, and they could actually do transfusions in the 1400s?"

"He talks about them using quills and reeds. Crude, but apparently effective. I suspect Professor Wilson will know."

"Is Darwin buying this?"

"Not really, he's just sitting back and listening." Bruce braked and made a sharp right. "Whew, almost missed the turn."

"Okay, on to the next question: the half man, half dragon creatures, his sons. How did that happen?"

"Turns out, it's a love story, a long one, but I'll cut to the chase. Zhao Yu had had many wives over the years, but they had all grown old and died, so when the white dragon was born, he gave his newest wife a transfusion as it slept, much like the one he had received from the red dragon. The problem was twofold. First, when the white dragon was born, its head was encrusted with barnacles, a strange species that had totally altered the dragon, making it incredibly powerful and crazy aggressive."

"And I thought the story was already weird. Yikes!"

Bruce chuckled. "Yes, and it was so aggressive that it began to terrorize anything and everything except for Zhao Yu and his young wife. And I mean everything. Animals, Fuegians, whales, a total rampage of killing, not for food, but for the fun of killing. The Fuegians, in their desperation, started building signal fires to warn of the approach of the dragon."

Luna interrupted him. "Wait, you mean that's why Tierra del Fuego is called Tierra del Fuego?"

"So it seems. A land of fire, indeed, but not caused by any fire-breathing dragon. Rather, the people running from it. Anyway, Zhao Yu tried everything he knew to control the dragon, and as a last resort managed to concoct a drug that would put the dragon to sleep, but only for periods of a few days."

"Weirder and weirder."

"Right, but it gets better still. The second problem was that his young wife was pregnant, unknown to him, and the blood of the dragon coursing through her, now somehow transmuted by the barnacles, resulted in the birth of two sons, one a live birth, a half man, half dragon, and the other in the form of a barnacle encrusted egg, supposedly with another half man inside."

"Wait, wait, wait. Live births, a woman laying an egg, cross species? That is medically impossible and bat shit crazy."

"Well, I would certainly think so, but—"

Luna groaned. "Remind me not to get pregnant."

"Indeed, because not surprisingly, she died in childbirth, or egg laying, if you will."

"And Darwin just sits there and says nothing? Bruce, I don't think I can take another minute of this."

"I understand, and no, Darwin objected, all right, and strenuously, but Zhao Yu was having none of it." Bruce slowed and turned into a parking space. "Well, here we are. I'll finish this on the ride home."

"Or not. I'm sure Professor Wilson will recognize a hoax when he sees one."

"But if it's real . . ."

"And it won't be, but if the world is off its axis, then we can talk about it on the ride to Bedford and Felmersham. If we have time, of course. The agent gave me a few listings to check out."

Bruce beamed at her. "Awesome!"

13

The City Mills, Haggerston, Penthouse, October 15, 2016, Morning.

Kat listened to the sounds of her coffee pot, a black Zojirushi, as it came to the end of its brewing cycle. *Sounds like Darth Vader gargling*, she thought.

She had completed her morning exercise routine in the home gym she had set up in one of her large unused bedrooms, and taken a long hot shower before throwing on a plush white robe and settling in for a well-earned cup of coffee and a hardboiled egg at the dining room table. The unopened box at the other end of the table caught her eye.

She knew what was inside: two bows recommended by Lars Andersen, a Danish archer she had met at a range near a shoot in Denmark. She couldn't believe the techniques he was using to shoot his arrows. Instead of drawing the bow with the arrow on the left side of the bow, as everyone does these days, he drew the bow with the arrows on the right, an ancient technique used by only a few archers in the world now. Using this method, he was able to get off several shots with incredible speed, almost like having an automatic bow. He could even do this on the run, seemingly combining Parkour with archery.

It was this combination that intrigued Kat. Luna really couldn't handle Parkour. Her eyesight just sucked too much. But she could run fairly fast, and Andersen's method, which allowed, even encouraged, shooting at close range, would be the perfect way to address Luna's vision problems. Instead of shooting at long range, she could run and shoot at shorter distances, even close up. It would be great fun.

If all went as planned, Kat would surprise Luna with the new bow on Monday and ask her to join her on a vacation in Denmark after the Scotland shoot. Andersen had agreed to give them a few lessons, and Kat didn't want to pass up this unique opportunity. Bruce was a complication, of course, but perhaps he could be coaxed into joining them. If not, Kat would go alone.

She took a sip of coffee, set her cup down, and padded barefoot into the kitchen to retrieve a sharp knife to deal with the packing tape. As she started back to the table, she noticed a flock of white birds circling and wheeling in the distance. *Gulls?*

One of the birds separated from the flock and sped toward Kat's building, growing larger and larger by the second. Kat dropped the knife and ran.

14

Room 2.30, Arts Building 2, Queen Mary, University of London, Mile End Road, London, October 15.

Professor Wilson's office was smaller than Luna expected but came with the usual trappings of professorship, including walls lined with books and a desk overcome by stacks of papers, the flotsam and jetsam of teaching and research. The room was brightly lit by the sun, so she kept her fedora and sunglasses on. The view from his one window was dismal: a cemetery of some sort, for whom, she didn't know, but it looked ancient. The room smelled like old books.

Professor Wilson noticed her reaction to the room. "A bit cramped, but it suits. Please, both of you, sit down." He motioned them into two wooden chairs on the other side of his desk. Nothing says welcome like a wooden chair, particularly a chair that squeaks loudly and wobbles when you sit down, but she guessed it was to keep student visits brief. It reminded her of the many times she had sat opposite professors at the University of Maryland, imploring them for a better grade or more time to complete a project. They had all listened carefully, and dutifully, and then quite firmly said "no."

The first thing Luna noticed about Wilson was his reaction to her, the familiar startle response of someone encountering a person with albinism. But, to his credit, he quickly welcomed her with a smile that was nothing less than endearing. He was shorter than Luna, with a bright round face, small brown eyes, almost beady, a neatly trimmed gray beard, and matching hair pulled back into a ponytail. He was fat to be sure, his blue corduroy vest serving more as a corset than clothing. He lowered himself into his chair with a grunt and gave them a hearty smile.

"Well, then," he said. "No time for pleasantries, I'm afraid. Can I see the documents in question?"

"Of course," said Bruce, placing copies of the letters and the journal on the desk, along with a piece of the shell.

Wilson pushed the shell fragment back across the desk. "Don't need this, not my field." He looked down at the documents. "These are obviously copies. Do you have the originals with you?"

"Yes, but—" Bruce began.

"Don't worry, young man, I only need to see them for a minute or so. Have to look at the paper and ink and judge their age."

Bruce reached into his bag and pulled out the originals, which made Professor Wilson's eyes grow large. "Oh, my. Oh, my, my, my."

Wilson took them from Bruce's hands and laid them carefully on the desk. "A moment, please." He reached into a drawer, pulled out a pair of pristine white gloves, and slipped them on. He measured the letters and the journal with a ruler, picked them up and sniffed them, and finally looked at the handwriting under a magnifying glass.

"What do you think?" said Bruce. "Are they fake?

Wilson paid no attention to the question, but spun in his chair to retrieve a book from his shelf. In his blue vest, he reminded

Luna of a giant globe of the world. He pulled the book down, thumbed through it, found the pages he was looking for, and placed the book on the desk so that Bruce and Luna could see. "Here's the genuine article, pages from a letter from Darwin to one of his sisters, Susan."

Bruce and Luna leaned in to look at the pages.

"So?" said Luna.

Wilson clapped his hands together and laid one of the letters next to the book. "See for yourself. The writing is absolutely identical. Plus, the paper is right, the ink is right, the letters are folded correctly, and the wax seal is perfect. Even the manner in which the letters are addressed, and to whom, is correct."

"You mean this is *real*?" said Luna, incredulous.

"Indeed," said Wilson. "Or I'm not a professor."

"But the story told in these letters and this journal is just—impossible," said Bruce. "Is there any chance at all that we're dealing with a clever forgery?"

Professor Wilson sighed and began pulling off his gloves. "I'd stake my reputation on it that these are one hundred percent genuine."

"Well, I'm staking my reputation—and job—on it, so I need to be absolutely sure," said Bruce. Luna nodded vigorously.

"You really need to read these documents," she said. "They're just—insane."

Professor Wilson sat back in his chair and crossed his arms. "Okay, here's what I can do. Leave a copy of all this with me and I'll read it through. If I'm not mistaken, Professor Smythe is in his office today, too. I'll see if I can have him take a look. If he agrees with me, we'll lock this down and button it up."

"That would be fantastic," said Bruce.

Professor Wilson handed the originals back to Bruce and stood to shake their hands. "How might I reach you later today?"

"We're on our way to do some house hunting," said Bruce. "Best to call me on my cell, my mobile." Bruce took a business card from his pocket and wrote down his cell number on the back.

Wilson took the card, glancing at the number. "Wonderful, I'll give you a call later today with whatever news I have. Good luck with the house hunting."

15

The Riverside Grill, Castle Lane, Bedford, October 15, Afternoon.

Luna and Bruce had driven to Bedford in near silence, each lost in their thoughts about the meeting with Professor Wilson. When Bruce had started in on the rest of Darwin's questions, Luna had stopped him, saying she'd had enough for one day and just wanted them to have a fun day looking at houses.

It was fun in a way, at least to Luna. She enjoyed seeing how other people lived, and some of the homes were beyond posh. On the other hand, and quite to her surprise, she and Bruce acted exactly the same as the couples they complained about on those home-buying television shows. He liked the grounds but not the house. Or she liked the foyer but hated the kitchen. Or they both hated the color of the paint, seeing it as an obstacle, even though it was an easy fix.

After the third house, they both threw up their hands and decided to stop for lunch, ending up at The Riverside Grill, in Bedford. She instantly liked it. Unlike the Victorian homes they'd been touring, the restaurant was perfectly modern, just like her apartment, with bright white walls and ceiling, contrasting black-lacquered chairs and tables set neatly on a polished taupe-colored concrete floor, bright red pendant lights dangling from the tall ceiling, and tall windows that wrapped around the restaurant, giving them a good view in just about any direction.

The maître d' had asked whether they wanted to sit on the heated terrace overlooking the River Ouse, but a strong cold breeze was blowing and it looked like rain, so they opted to sit inside, at a small table near two tall exotic-looking purple-leafed trees, and enjoy the smells coming from the kitchen, which were intoxicating.

Luna had chosen the shredded duck salad, and Bruce had gone for the Thai curry chicken dish with coconut rice, and the food was so good, each insisted on sharing their meals. *You must taste this!*

The waiter had cleared everything away now, and they had both decided against dessert or coffee, so as they waited for the check, they quietly sipped what was left of their wine, a house white with surprisingly noble character—no Duct Tape Chardonnay here—and stared out the window.

"Shall we press on to Felmersham, then?" she asked.

Bruce gave her a little frown. "I'd just as soon—"

His cell phone rang, and he pulled it out of his pocket just in time to take the call. "Hello. Yes, professor, glad you were able to reach me, but you're breaking up a bit. Let me go outside."

He stood and motioned for Luna to remain seated. "I'll be right back. Enjoy your wine."

Bruce walked quickly to the door and stepped outside. "Hello, professor."

"Can you hear me now?"

"Yes, go on, were you able to reach Professor Smythe?"

"Yes, indeed, and he agrees with me. The documents are genuine, in our opinion, without question. Darwin has even rewarded us with some of his common spelling errors. He should never have entered a spelling bee, I can tell you that. His sister Catherine was always on him about that, and—"

"But what the letters and journal say—that story—it's just beyond belief."

"It is, um, *unusual*, I'll give you that. On the other hand, all the facts—except for the dragons and cross-species nonsense, of course—fit with what Darwin did once he got home, especially his intense study of barnacles. Why, it might even add a new twist to why he delayed publication of his master work."

"But that kooky story . . ."

"Mr. Cargo, look at it this way. Are you a fan of Sherlock Holmes by chance?"

"I've read some of his books, yes. Elementary, my dear Watson and all of that."

"Well, here's how I think Holmes would answer you. It's a quotation I use every year with my students: *When you've eliminated the impossible, whatever remains, however improbable, must be the truth.*"

"So the dragons and half dragons?"

"Impossible, of course, and I think it's safe to say that Darwin would agree with that. On the other hand, given that the story is coming from none other than Charles Darwin, and that he took such pains to record his interaction with Zhao Yu, perhaps all the rest is merely improbable."

"What next, then, from your perspective?"

"It's all about the barnacles and that egg. You'll need to follow up with an appropriate expert for that. On the other hand . . ."

"Yes?"

"Smythe and I would like to work with you on a paper for publication in—"

Bruce interrupted him. "That's not for me to say, Professor. The Survey will decide how this discovery will be announced, I'm afraid."

"Well, at least keep that thought in mind. It would be an honor to work with you."

"I'll do that professor. In the meantime, I have to ask that you not discuss this with anyone without first talking with me."

"As you wish."

"And I would like very much that you keep that copy in a safe place. I'll be around to collect it."

"Of course, no problem. And while you're at it, you can collect the shell fragment you left behind."

Bruce had forgotten about it. "Yes, I will."

They said their goodbyes and Bruce walked back into the restaurant. Luna was just signing the credit card slip, as well as an autograph for their waiter, who had been unusually attentive during the meal. Now Bruce knew why.

"What's up?" she said.

Bruce took a deep breath, and sighed. She wasn't going to like this.

"Well, that's a heavy sigh," she said. "Go on, tell me."

"Smythe agrees with Wilson. It's all real."

"But the story, surely —"

Luna's cell phone began ringing. She pulled it out of her pocket and hit the talk button.

"Yes? Wait, slow down. Kat? Kat, what? Kat, you're scaring me! Slow down! Oh, my god, are you all right? Yes, yes, I understand. We're in Bedford, so it will be a while. But we're on our way. Yes, tell the constable that. Bye."

"What the hell?" said Bruce. *"Constable?"*

Luna shook her head, trying to understand. "It was Kat. My apartment has been tossed, and Kat sounded . . . *terrified.*"

16

Room 2.30, Arts Building 2, Queen Mary, University of London, Mile End Road, London, October 15, 2016, Afternoon.

Professor Wilson pulled the copies of the Darwin documents together, evened out the pages with a tap on his desk, and put them into a folder before slipping them into the top drawer of his desk. He noticed that Cargo hadn't taken the egg fragment with him. He picked it up, held it up to the light, and gave it a cursory glance. *I have no idea.* He opened his desk drawer and dropped it in.

The call had not gone as well as he had hoped, but perhaps this Cargo fellow would have a change of heart. I mean, after all, he had few peers when it came to the study of Darwin. Maybe he should go directly to Cargo's boss. He was sure he could find the name online. *No*, he thought, *better give the man some time. A week, say.*

A gust of wind rattled the window.

It happened so fast. First the sound of shattering glass, then the feeling of being grasped by something powerful beyond measure, its talons sinking into him, tearing at him, pulling him apart, the pain intense then dropping away entirely as he caught flashes of scales and teeth and blood. He had the sense of tumbling through the air, a boy again, practicing his forward rolls on the lawn, the world right side up, then upside down—sky, ground, sky, ground—on and on as the world went from dim to dark and then exploded in brightness to the high-pitched wail of countless voices. He didn't know whether to go to the light or run away. In the end, it didn't matter. He was the light, he was the sound, and he knew that he would sing this song forever.

PART TWO

And so it was that Zhu Di, the Yongle Emperor, fell ill in the Gobi, chasing the Tartar horde, and died in his tent from seizures three, each robbing him of faculties, the last of life. His funeral was magnificent in pomp, with thirty fair maidens hanged to accompany him in death. Many watched, but the wise fled, the wrath of succession to avoid, the Red Dragon and his guardians among them, disappearing like ghosts in darkest night to bide their time and preserve their might.
— Zhang Wei, *The Emperor's Dragons* (1513)

17

Darwin's Study, Down House, Downe, 4:00 p.m., Monday, April 24, 1882.

Charles Darwin had been dead for five days, but it seemed to Lily that Down House itself had died with him. Clocks had been silenced, their hands positioned to display the time of death. Mirrors had been covered, an action — so the superstition went — that prevented the deceased's image from getting trapped within it. Covering the mirror was also said to protect anyone who might look into it, an action that would identify them as next to die. Worst of all, to Lily's mind, was seeing all the family photographs placed face down, the superstition being that it protected the family and other mourners from being possessed by the spirit of the dead.

Lily had been sitting in Darwin's darkened study for about half an hour, the curtains drawn as part of the mourning ritual. Henrietta, Darwin's oldest daughter, known to all as Etty, dressed head to toe in black, had shown her into the room, placing a single candle on Darwin's desk and motioning Lily into his favorite wingchair. Etty had then turned on her heels, promising to return as soon as she could.

Even in the dim light, Lily could make out the room's every detail. His cluttered desk, his wonderful roller chair that had so delighted the children, his full bookcases, and the many specimens he had collected over the years. She had spent hours upon hours here, being poked and measured and asked to perform her transformation over and over again, so that Darwin might capture every detail in his little notebooks.

Lily turned at the sound of the door squeaking open. Etty walked in and quickly closed the door, the arc of outside light disappearing, the room darkening once more.

She got right to the point. "She doesn't want to see you, at least not now."

"I know she's busy, but—"

"It's not being busy. She just doesn't—"

"Want to see me. Yes, I understand that, but I simply must talk to her."

Etty shook her head, and sighed. "Perhaps I can help. What is it that you want? Why have you come back after so many years?" She paused, wondering whether to continue. "And why, why on earth have you not aged a day since I last saw you?"

Lily rolled her eyes. "I came back to get what I want, and I would have thought that by now you would have known all that there is to know about me . . . from your father."

Etty gave her head a quick shake. "He said very little about you after you left. Every question was ignored or rebuffed, so you remain a mystery to me."

"And that's probably for the best."

Etty huffed. "But why?"

Lily stood and took Etty's hands in hers. "Enough questions. Let me tell you what I want, and if you can help, I'll be gone. You need never see me again."

Etty pulled her hands away, and sighed. "It's not that I want you gone."

"But your mother does, and I will respect that. Now, tell me where the notebooks are."

"The notebooks?"

"The ones about me. There are six of them, I believe, and I know he used to keep them locked here in this desk. They are small and green and held shut by bronze clasps. And there are labels on them, L1 through L6."

Etty nodded. "I asked about the locked drawer more than once. You may not know this, but I helped him pull together his books. Editing and so forth. And I always wondered whether he was keeping something important from me."

"So we just need the key."

Etty bit her lip. "I don't know. That would be something for mother to decide."

"But she won't see me. It's up to you."

Etty shook her head, firm in her resolve. "No, I will have to ask mother." She turned toward the door. "Wait here, I'll be right back."

Etty opened the door and was gone.

18

The City Mills, Haggerston, Apartment 132.

Constable James Harris couldn't keep his eyes off Kat. She was so amazingly beautiful. He knew he'd seen her somewhere, on the telly perhaps, but couldn't quite place her. Ever since his arrival, he'd been trying to calm her down, at least enough for her to make a coherent statement. She kept talking about "a monster," which wasn't helping one bit.

He'd been in the area, part of his duties as a member of the Haggerston local policing team, and had been first on the scene. Kat had been standing at the door to the flat, which he had determined was not hers, clearly terrified. Not much had happened since. She had managed a call to the flat owner, one Luna Fearnow, and the crime scene investigators, led by Hermione Divers, had arrived and begun their work.

It looked to Harris like just another house-breaking, one of a couple hundred so far this year, but the odd thing was the method of entrance into the flat. It wasn't every day that a thief broke in to a ninth-storey flat, especially from the outside, and with such force. Then again, it would be nice to have a cat burglar for a change.

He tried talking to Kat again. "Miss Murphy, do you think we could talk now?"

She looked up at him from the chair he had found for her just inside the door to the flat. As scared as she was, she was still a woman, and the man standing over her now was definitely in the wheelhouse of her requirements for a man: tall, strong, handsome, a bright smile, eyes that seemed to penetrate you. She took a deep breath. "I think so."

"Good, good, no rush, though. Just go over with me what happened, from the time you became aware of the break-in."

Kat nodded and tugged her robe closed at the neck, blocking his view of her breasts, which he was clearly fixated on, for good reason. "I was eating breakfast. I'd gone to the kitchen to get a knife. I just got a new bow in the post and I wanted to check it out."

A new bow. Perhaps she was a musician. He couldn't help but imagine her legs wrapped around a cello. "Yes, and then?"

A shiver went through her. "I saw — I saw — *something* flying toward the building. At first I thought it was a bird, a seagull or something, but it just kept getting larger and larger, until . . ."

Oh, no, here we go again with the monster, he thought. "Take your time, Miss Murphy."

"You don't believe me, I know it," she said, choking back tears. "But I *know* what I saw."

"Yes, madam, the *monster* you talked about earlier."

"At first I thought it was coming to *my* apartment, so I ran to my bedroom and bolted the door."

"But it wasn't."

"No, I could tell that whatever it was, it had broken in to my friend Luna's apartment. I heard glass shattering, and then there were thumping noises for some minutes, and then nothing. So, when the noises stopped, I came out of my room, and there it was again, flying away. I grabbed Luna's spare key — we share those just in case — and came down to take a look at . . . *this*." She waved her arm at the room. "I was *so relieved* she wasn't here."

Tables, chairs, and sofas were overturned. Cabinets were open. Drawers had been emptied and tossed aside. Cooking pots and broken dishes were scattered over the kitchen floor. There were huge slashes in every piece of furniture with fabric. Whatever the thief was after, he was intent on finding it. Most impressive, and unusual, was the sheer destruction of the door to the patio. The door and its frame had been shattered utterly, creating an opening big enough for a bull moose to walk through. This was no cat burglar's quiet, artful cutting of glass, but the work of something approaching a battering ram.

Constable Harris nodded. "Okay, miss, you sit right here a bit. I'm sure Miss Fearnow will be along shortly."

Kat sighed. "You *still* don't believe me, do you?"

"It's not what I believe, miss. It's what the crime scene investigators and the rest of the team turn up. We'll be interviewing neighbors in this building and anyone in other buildings who might have had a clear view of the—of the *monster*—and of course we'll be looking at videos from the nearest CCTV cameras. Not much escapes our attention." That wasn't exactly true, but he thought it was a good thing to say, anyway.

"Good, good," she said, seeming more confident now. "You'll see I'm right."

"Indeed, madam." *Who was she?* It was driving him mad. "Excuse me for a moment. I need to talk to the CSI lead. When I get back, perhaps you can describe in detail what this—this monster—as you say, looked like."

19

The City Mills, Haggerston, Apartment 132.

Hermione Divers, lead CSI investigator, pulled off her gloves and walked over to Constable Harris.

"What have you learned from the girl, James?" she said. "Still sticking to her monster story?"

"Indeed."

"Well, something big and powerful burst into this flat, so *monster* may not be a bad term."

Harris shook his head. "I think the videos and reports from neighbors will tell a different story."

"I hope so, but I also wonder."

"Wonder?"

"Do you know how much force it takes to break through a door frame and window like that?"

Harris smirked. "You're going to tell me, aren't you?" Sometimes her analyses and statistics were just too much to bear.

She was a short reed of a woman, almost anorexic and plain as a wall, with close-cropped brown hair, hazel eyes, and a way of moving about a crime scene in her CSI togs that suggested a cat on the prowl. She was forever squinting at the details, evidence bags and tweezers at the ready. For all that, she was also the best forensic specialist he had ever encountered.

Divers smiled back at him. "I like to be precise in my work, James, you should know that by now. It's how I roll, but this — this *violence* — is off the charts. I mean, we're talking about a force akin to being hit by a cement lorry."

Harris looked over at the mangled door frame and the gaping hole. "Maybe there was more than one burglar, a team say, with sledge hammers?"

Divers came out with a sound that seemed to surpass a guffaw. "Oh, shit, James, there's not enough room on that little patio to accommodate the number of men it would take to accomplish this. Even then it would take hours."

Harris shrugged. "Well, what then?"

Divers looked around the apartment, squinting. "I'm thinkin' a monster, James, a real brute of a monster."

It was the first time he had heard her giggle, albeit in a professional way.

20

The City Mills, Haggerston, Apartment 132.

Hermione Divers had just about finished up her work when Luna and Bruce arrived, Kat immediately jumping into Luna's arms and crying, Bruce looking wide-eyed at the damage to the apartment. Hermione stepped into the hall to take a call, motioning to Harris to take over.

"Holy Christ," Bruce said. "Who could have done this?"

Constable Harris introduced himself. "And you are?"

"Sorry," Bruce said, "I'm Bruce Cargo—the boyfriend. The apartment's hers." He nodded toward Luna.

"Right, then, I may have a few questions for you, but right now I need to talk to Ms. Fearnow. This is still an active crime scene, so could I ask you to step into the hall a moment?"

"Of course." Bruce gave Luna a little wave and stepped back into the hallway.

Luna nodded and guided Kat back into the chair. "I won't be a minute, Kat. It's all going to be fine, I promise."

"Luna, they won't listen to me. I *know* what I saw."

Luna could see the constable shaking his head. "Well, I'll listen to you, Kat. Just let me talk to the constable a second."

She turned to survey the room. *Shit, it's a total wreck!* She shook her head and extended her hand. "I'm Luna Fearnow.

Looks like we've got quite a mess. What happened? Or do you know yet?"

Constable Harris sighed. "Constable Harris, madam. I've been on the scene since Ms. Murphy called 999."

"And what have you got?"

"Well, what's clear from our initial inspection and the work of CSI is that someone with considerable strength broke into your flat, smashing through the patio door and, as you can see, pretty much giving your flat a right tumble."

"And what is it that Kat says she saw that you seem to discount?"

Harris looked down at Kat and then back at Luna. "She said she saw a monster, a flying monster."

A chill went up Luna's spine. She looked at Kat, who was nodding vigorously, on the verge of tears again. "Constable Harris, this monster, by any chance did it appear to be part human and part—I know this will sound strange, but I have to say it—part *dragon*?"

"Yes!" Kat said. "That's what I saw!"

Constable Harris wasn't sure what to say. "Why would you say that?"

Before Luna could answer, Hermione stuck her head back in the room and interrupted. "James, I've got to go. All that remains to do here is have the owners look for anything missing. I'm on a new call. Another break-in just like this one, on the Queen Mary campus, but it looks to be a homicide, too."

"The Queen Mary campus?" said Bruce, stepping back into the apartment. "We were just there this morning to see Professor Wilson."

Hermione gave him an odd look and glanced at her notebook. "Professor Simon Wilson, Arts Building Two?"

21

The Gladstone, Number 6, Finsbury Park, Sunday Morning, October 16.

Pontius Pibb awoke to the scratchy licks of his cat, Lucifer, a short-haired black cat, age six, whose biological clock suggested that Pibb had slept far longer than necessary. *Too many bloody pints at the Faltering Fullback*, he thought.

Admittedly, he was still in shock over the news story that had popped up on the television screen. He had watched gobsmacked as file images of Luna and that other model, Kat Murphy, were interspersed with blurry images of something—some flying thing—caught on several different CCTV cameras, as well as some mobile phone videos already creating a buzz on YouTube.

He had called it a night, paid his tab, and gone home in a pissing rain to his small flat near the stadium, a dream location for an Arsenal fan, and cheap enough, though prices seemed to be climbing with the steady influx of young people looking for a remedy to the outrageous pricing of downtown London. *It's good to have a job.*

As soon as he had walked in the door, he had flipped on the telly, switching from channel to channel to follow the story. It had only been hours, but the media were having a right field day with the story, each channel doing its bloody best to outdo the others, their twisted story leads and scrolls changing by the minute:

Murder Most Foul at Queen Mary
Strange Beast Loose in London
Supermodels Implicated in University Murder
Lesbian Love Nest Disturbed by Rampaging Beast
There Be Dragons in Haggerston
Dragon Man May Be Elaborate Scheme to Promote New Film
Models Create Bizarre Story to Cover Up Murder
Police Stumped by Dragon Man
Dragon Man: Real, Hoax, or Promotional Gimmick?
Aging Model Using Hoax to Jumpstart Career?
Albinos and Dragons, Oh My!

He turned his head and gave Lucifer a weary look. "A classic case of Powell's Law, Luci: *If any statement can be screwed up in a way to disquiet the public, it will be screwed up.*"

The story was already the darling of late night talk shows and hurriedly assembled special reports, and seemed to be picking up interest from the States as well. He could only imagine what the morning papers would say. The headlines would be huge, and screaming.

Pibb grabbed the zapper and switched to a talk show. A university professor was explaining the origins of dragon myths. "Every culture makes reference to dragons, so who's to say we're not dealing with an actual dragon? I mean, take the orangutan as just one example. It's been around for over 400,000 years, but it was a myth until it was discovered in the seventeenth century." *Rubbish*, Pibb thought.

He switched channels again. A computer expert was explaining how easy it would be to hack a CCTV camera and create what looked like a real video. "The fact is today's technology can create anything it wants, whenever it wants." *What about the bloody mobile videos, you git?*

He changed the channel. A police inspector was pushing aside cameras as he walked to his car. Confident. Arrogant. Pibb liked him immediately.

"We have an ongoing investigation," the man said. "When we know something, you'll know something." With that, Pibb had clicked off the telly and gone to bed.

The early morning light was streaming in the window now. No sign of last night's rain. He yawned, gave Lucifer a scratch under the chin, and climbed out of bed. There was only one tin of cat food on the shelf.

"Oh, Luci, you'll be so happy to know I've found a job. Or at least I hope I still have a job after this — *mess*. Tomorrow should be a very interesting day."

He opened the tin and dumped the food into Lucifer's bowl. "Here you go, mate."

The cat started feasting, which made Pibb's stomach rumble. "I'm hungry as you, Luci. Could put away a full English this morning, I could."

He checked the fridge, which was near empty. Maybe Miss Fearnow could spot him an advance, so he could do a proper shopping at the supermarket. "Well, bollocks, looks like my fry-up will be a sausage and an egg."

22

Scotland Yard, Curtis Green Building, Victoria Embankment, London, Sunday Morning, October 16.

Hermione Divers did not like being interrogated on her methods and results, but it was part of the job, and she knew the only way to get through this without leaping over the desk and strangling her superior was to answer his questions precisely and concisely. It did not help that their history had been combative from the start.

"And when will these DNA results on the tooth be ready, Divers?" said Detective Chief Inspector Roger Falvey, head of the Murder/Major Investigation Unit for the area.

It was maddening how much he didn't listen to the details. "Not a tooth sir. A piece of a claw or talon."

"Whatever. When then?"

She resisted responding to the tone in his voice. "About a week, perhaps less." *There's that bloody smirk again.*

As much as she loathed him, she had to admit that he was a fine specimen of a man, tall and muscular, mid-forties, with the looks of some goddam model and steel blue eyes that would melt the knickers off of most women. Until you got to know him, of course. If she were being kind, and she was not about to be, she would say he was just brusque. But if she were to be honest, which was her true nature, she'd have to say he was just an arsehole in full flame. And what made matters worse was that he just didn't realize it, or didn't care.

"Let's try for 'perhaps less,' shall we?"

"Yes, sir."

"And the CCTV images?"

"Real as far as we can tell to this point, but we're not through with them quite yet. And to answer your next question, Monday afternoon, I would think."

Falvey gave her a menacing look. "On your best, Divers, we're all on the same team here." *Are we?* It seemed to him, at least this morning, that everyone was on a different team, from the mayor to the deputy mayor, to the Mayor's Office on Policing and Crime, to the London Assembly Police and Crime, and to every other bloody person and entity that had him here in this office on a Sunday morning. The order of the day seemed to be damage control, not criminal investigation. He wouldn't be surprised if the next person to give him a call was the bloody prime minister.

"Yes sir, sorry sir."

"What about the method of breaking and entering? Any final conclusions?"

Divers sighed. "We've decided that the amount of force required to mangle the patio door and create an entrance of those dimensions *could* have—could have been—accomplished by any number of force-multiplying devices. Cables and pulleys and such."

He rapped his knuckles on the desk. "So, all this monster talk is, in fact, nonsense."

"Not quite, sir. The problem is, whichever force multiplier one uses would require attachments and cabling inside the flat in order to pull that door down. So, to gain entry, whoever or whatever would already have to be in the flat. And what's the point of that?"

Falvey rocked back in his chair and began rubbing his temples. It was going to be a long day. "And what about the other one, the murder scene?"

"Same mode of entry, blunt force, but not near the force needed. It was just a plain old double-hung wooden window."

"So we could be looking at two unrelated crimes?"

"I suppose that's possible, but given the condition of the body, I'd say we're dealing with a murderer of considerable strength." She placed a folder in front of him. "Here are the crime scene photos."

Falvey opened the folder and almost immediately looked away. "Good God!"

"It was quite a mess, I must admit. Blood everywhere, spray patterns like a Jackson Pollock painting. The poor man was literally torn apart."

Falvey quickly flipped through the other photographs, then closed the folder. "Weapons?"

"Sharp instrument, consistent with multiple scalpels, but most probably claws or talons. The examiner will have more to say, I'm sure, but it looked like the murderer did a breast stroke through the victim."

"Breast stroke?"

"Like in swimming, sir." She stood and demonstrated the stroke, both arms together coming forward, and then a stroke to the outside. "He or it plunged its hands or whatever into the victim's chest and then just literally tore him apart, and then kept at it for some seconds. Biggest piece we found was his head, or at least part of it."

Falvey shook his head. "And we're sure this is Professor Wilson?"

Divers nodded. "Not my territory, but I was there when his associates were questioned at the scene. They identified him from his head and his blue vest. We're sure it's him."

"Okay, fine. Look, I'm calling a team briefing for tomorrow morning at 8:00. I'd like you or someone from the Evidence Recovery Unit to bring us up to speed on what we know by then."

"Yes, sir, I'll be ready."

"Fine, then. On your way out, give DI Morton a shout and send him in."

"Yes, sir," she said, relieved to be on her way.

23

The City Mills, Haggerston, Penthouse, Sunday Morning, October 16.

Kat looked back and forth between Luna and Bruce. They were both so quiet.

They had surprised her, arriving half an hour early, just as she had finished dressing for the day ahead: wide-bottomed black jeans, a white crocheted shell top under a camel suede fringed waistcoat, and open-toed brown ankle boots. Maybe too dressy for breakfast but not for what she had planned—some shopping and a late lunch with a Luna-approved photographer eager to work with her. Luna had given her a look of approval when she had arrived, but Kat knew she didn't approve of open-toed shoes in such cool weather. *Whatever.*

Luna, it seemed, was going to have another black-on-black day, with classically tailored slacks and matching short jacket over a cream-colored blouse. Bruce was in his "uniform," old jeans and a long-sleeved black Henley jersey. *What could he be thinking?* Kat thought.

She put down her fork. "So . . . do you like it?"

Her words startled them. They were both lost in thought over what had transpired the past twenty-four hours.

"It's wonderful, Kat," said Luna, taking another bite of her American biscuits and gravy.

"Truly," said Bruce. "The cheese grits are perfect."

Kat beamed. "Thank you, thank you, it's the least I could do after yesterday. And if you really want a great Georgia breakfast, y'all will just have to come with me to Atlanta next summer. The yoghurt pancakes and hash browns at Sweet Melissa's in Decatur are to die for, and the strawberries with fresh-made whipped cream at The Original Pancake House are just out of this world."

"Tell you what," said Luna. "You'll have to swing by Berkeley Springs with me for some *real* hash browns at Earth Dog Café. They're loaded with onions, the absolute best."

Bruce threw up his hands. "Sorry, I have nothing to offer, but if you're done, could we talk a little about yesterday?"

Luna put down her biscuit. "Well, I for one am *pissed*."

"At me?" said Kat, looking stricken.

"No, of course not, Kat. The police, the media — the fucking media! The things they're saying."

Bruce reached over and took her hand. "Luna, this will all go away once the police make a statement. We're all victims here."

"Well, you'd never know it from the way we've been treated. I don't fucking like the way they cross-examined us, like we were the monster, and the media, they're, they're —"

"They're just doing their job," said Bruce, quickly adding, "except for the media, that is. They're fucking out of control."

Luna slumped back in her chair and crossed her arms under her breasts. "Well, I don't like it."

"I'm pissed, too," said Kat. "At myself, mostly."

"Why, for heaven's sake?" said Bruce.

"I was so weak. I just ran in terror. And then bawled all day like a baby."

"Oh, Kat, I would have done the same thing, I'm sure," said Luna. "If I'd seen it, I probably would have peed my pants."

Kat managed a giggle. "It *was* terrifying, but not next time. Next time, I'll be shooting arrows."

"Let's hope there is no next time," said Bruce. "But since we're having a pissed party, add me in to the mix. Taking the documents and shell fragments from me as "evidence" was just wrong, and it may cost me my job. When Old Nozzle hears about it, I'll be toast."

"Well, at least you had the good sense to scan the documents on Friday," said Luna. "We at least have that. Friday — it seems so long ago."

"So what now?" Kat asked.

Bruce glanced at his watch. "We'd better be on our way. Wouldn't want to keep Detective Inspector Morton waiting. Maybe I can convince him to give me my stuff back."

"Well, I'm looking forward to it," said Kat.

Luna frowned. "What?"

"Working with the artist."

"Oh, that should be fun," said Luna. "Make sure you get a copy. I want to see what we're dealing with. Those blurry images they're showing on television are just pathetic. Looks like a blob with wings."

Kat shuddered. "A blob it wasn't."

24

The Gladstone, Number 6, Finsbury Park, Sunday Evening, October 16.

Pibb opened the second tin of cat food for the day and dropped it into Lucifer's bowl. "Well, I hope you're happy with yourself, matey, 'cause you're getting the best this evening."

The trip to the supermarket had been frustrating. He could only afford two tins of cat food and a day-old sandwich wrapped in plastic. The sandwich had been nasty, and he'd set it aside after just two bites, the second bite taken to make sure he'd interpreted the taste correctly with the first bite. He had.

"Here you go, Luci." He put the bowl on the floor, and Lucifer pounced on it. "It's going to be a lean week, old boy. Treats on Friday, though, I promise." Perhaps sooner if his new boss was amenable to a small advance.

He went to the fridge and took out a beer. "Woe is me, Luci. Well, let's see what the media have been up to."

He slumped down in front of the telly, grabbed the flipper, and turned on the set. The first image, which came so unexpectedly he jumped, precious beer flying everywhere, was a clip of Luna laying a right good roundhouse punch on the nose of a reporter, the man out cold before he hit the ground.

"Oh, my, that's my new boss, Luci. Jolly good for her!"

The rest was just jerky camera footage of her, the other model, and some guy jostling their way from a building to a car, reporters and onlookers in frenzied pursuit, including a crazed woman with a sign that read THE END IS NEAR.

"Oh, hell no," Pibb said. "I just got a bloody fuckin' job."

25

Briefing Room 3, Scotland Yard, Monday Morning, October 17.

Hermione Divers was just wrapping up her presentation. She took a deep breath. The whole room smelled of testosterone.

"So, in summary, here's what we have. One, the murderer entered both locations with preternatural force, more force than can be logically accounted for using any other method of entry. Two, the CCTV images captured at both locations, however blurry, are consistent with a single perpetrator. Three, hair analyses at both locations indicate the presence of two albinos, Ms. Fearnow, of course, and one other, and the same hairs were at both scenes. So again, we appear to be looking at one perpetrator—we'll nail that down when the DNA reports come back. Four, according to Ms. Fearnow, the only items missing from her flat were copies of letters and a journal purported to be written by none other than Charles Darwin himself, the content of which mentions a monster consistent with the images shown on the CCTV cameras. Five, it appears that the only items taken from Professor Wilson's office were copies of those selfsame documents, plus a fragment said to be from a dragon's egg. Sixth, and finally, the hairs and the broken talon are now undergoing DNA analysis, along with egg fragments provided by Mr. Cargo. We should have the results later this week, perhaps sooner — these samples are definitely being given top priority by Forensic Services. And I think that's about it. Questions?"

An officer in the back of the room raised his hand. "Sergeant Tompkins here. A question about the CCTV images. They're very blurry, more blurry than usual. Why is that?"

"Good question, Sergeant, and the answer is that most of the blurriness is due to the speed of whatever that was flying about. We've calculated its speed at about 385 kilometers an hour, or about the speed of a diving Peregrine Falcon."

"Wow, so maybe my next question is moot. I was just wondering, we know we've all seen sky divers and such, some sporting fabric wings of a sort. Could that be what's going on?"

Hermione shook her head. "No, for one thing, the speed is just not possible, unless death is your goal, plus anyone using such equipment would only be able to brake using a parachute of some kind, and that's not what happened here. What we have here is very hawk-like: a quick dive and an equally quick stop, all using powerful wings. And just to reiterate my earlier comments, we're working now to sharpen those images — should have something for you later today."

Hermione looked around the room. "Any other questions?"

The room remained silent.

"Thank you, and again, I'll let you know as soon as we hear anything from the DNA analysis." She moved from behind the lectern and took a seat, giving way to Detective Chief Inspector Falvey.

"All right, then," he said. "First off, I wanted to share our artist's image of what Ms. Murphy has alleged she saw." He motioned to a sergeant at the back of the room to kill the lights. He grabbed the zapper and clicked it, the image popping up quickly. Some in the room gasped, others laughed, but most just shook their heads.

Falvey picked up a laser pointer and began pointing out the features of the image. "So, gentlemen, even though our CCTV images are lacking a bit and show only bits of wing, as you can see, Ms. Murphy described in detail a beast half man and half dragon. A somewhat distorted human face, maybe Chinese, but with a long snout, pointed ears, and strange bumps on its forehead. Long white hair. Its torso is large and appears to have scales of some kind, particularly along its back. Its arms seem to be somewhat longer than normal, and quite muscular, with large hands and what looks like talon-tipped fingers. Its feet, if you can call them that, appear to be more like claws, and only four-toed, one of which springs from the heel—very odd. Last, the wings are large, almost bat-like, and reportedly translucent. And yes, perfectly white, like an albino."

He indicated to the sergeant to turn on the lights. "So, any questions?"

An officer in the front row raised a hand. "Two questions, sir. First, how can Ms. Murphy provide such a clear description when the thing she saw, whatever she saw, was moving so fast?"

Falvey turned to Divers and motioned her to take the question. She stood and faced the officer.

"Ms. Murphy was positioned in such a way as to have a clear view of the thing as it was slowing down to land on the patio just below her penthouse flat." She sat down.

"Okay, one last question, and I don't mean to take issue with all that's been presented here this morning, but sir, can this be anything other than a hoax? I mean, come on. Look at the size of that John Thomas. Sounds like wishful thinking on the part of Ms. Murphy." Everyone laughed except Divers, who rolled her eyes, and Falvey, who gave the officer a withering look.

"Officer, I certainly hope that this whole thing is a hoax, but our approach will be serious and thorough, including yours. Do I make myself clear?"

The officer nodded sheepishly. "Yes, sir."

"First off, then, no one, and I mean no one, is to mention this artist's sketch or make it available to anyone. Second, consistent with the evidence reported by Divers and the in-depth interviews of Fearnow, Cargo, and Murphy, who all told consistent stories, we've eliminated them as possible suspects. DI Morton will be briefing you on your assignments momentarily, but the lines of inquiry we'll be following, at least until we have DNA results, will be three. First, we need to gather any other images we can find of the murderer—and we'll call him that for now, not beast or monster or dragon-man. That means mobile phone videos and anything on social media. DI Morton will be assigning a team for that. A second team will follow up on what we will call the second albino. Who could he be? Why was he in both locations? Is he the murderer? Finally, a third team, led by DI Morton himself, will be looking into the authenticity of the documents in question with an eye for determining whether we are indeed dealing with a hoax. You should note here that in the interviews of Fearnow and Cargo, both mentioned that Professor Wilson, an expert on Darwin, thought the documents were genuine. They also said that Wilson involved a Professor Smythe at Queen Mary to get a second opinion. The interesting thing here is that there is no record of a Professor Smythe at Queen Mary. Why?"

He scanned the room. "Okay, then, Mr. Morton, they're all yours." With that, Falvey walked from the room. The whole room seemed to heave a sigh of relief at his parting.

DI Harry Morton stood and moved to the front of the room. Falvey may have been more handsome, at least in Divers' mind, but Morton had a presence about him. When you worked with him, you knew you'd close the case. His analytical skills were legend, and they all came in a plain and friendly package everyone but newcomers called Harry. He was just under six feet tall, barrel-chested and sturdy, with a salt-and-pepper crewcut long out of style. His eyes were an orangish brown, nothing special, but you didn't want to be on the receiving end of them in an interview room. The nose inserted between them had clearly seen a fist or two, the flesh going this way and that before finally pointing off to the left. He always seemed to need a shave, but never had a beard, and it was a rare day when you saw him in anything other than a brown tweed sports jacket over a plaid shirt with a plain tie, usually coffee brown, though he had once been reported to wear a Christmas tie. His usual look was serious, even pensive, which made his smile even more disarming when you were lucky to see one. These usually came at the end of a case with the clinking of glasses at the local pub.

"All right, lads, I'll be calling out the members of each team, which I will meet with separately after this briefing, so stay close. That includes you, Divers, if you don't mind. One point of caution for all of you. No talking to the press. And not just about the sketch. I mean no talking whatsoever. Period. They already seem to be out of control, so let's not make matters worse."

Detective Tompkins raised his hand again. "What is it, Fred?"

"I was just wondering, Harry. Are we in this alone or will we have to deal with other agencies?"

"For now, we're alone, but you know as well as I do that if we don't solve this thing quickly, every bloody agency in the country will be involved, including intelligence and the military. The media are just putting on too much pressure."

He scanned the room. "Any other questions aside from the size of that thing's todger?"

Everyone laughed. "Good then, let's begin."

26

Outside the Preston-Manfred Agency, London, Monday, October 17.

The ride in with Kat had been hair-raising but thankfully uneventful, at least once they had raced through the throng of reporters outside the apartment building. It was unclear whether the obscenities Kat had shouted or the injurious potential presented by two women in a fast-moving clown car had done the trick, but the seas had parted and they had been on their way, Kat's radio blaring another oldie, "American Woman," by Lenny Kravitz.

Half an hour later, Kat pulled up behind the shiny limousine parked in front of the agency building. She looked over at Luna, who was massaging her right hand. "So how is it this morning?"

"Bloody awful, hurts like hell."

"You should be seen."

"Maybe, but too much to do today, and as much as it hurts, it's way better than last night."

Kat nodded toward the people standing beside the limousine. "Is that your Mr. Pibb there in the uniform?"

Luna smiled at the sight of Mr. Pibb standing next to Ahmed Abhoud, one in a somewhat wrinkled chauffeur's uniform, the other in a shiny black Armani suit. "Yes, that's him."

"Not bad, actually, but who's this other man you've kept secret from me? He's Omar Sharif *gorgeous*."

Luna had to agree. Ahmed was as well put together as any man she had ever seen. Perhaps too well. She liked his face and his lean, toned body, but he was too much of a clothes horse for her tastes. His suit, his tie, his shoes, his neatly folded handkerchief—all impeccable, elegant, and overdone. It was as if he were a model getting ready for another *GQ* shoot. And she really didn't care for male models. And something else. She didn't know quite what, but there was something disingenuous about the way he treated her, the way he looked at her. As seemingly sweet as he had been to her, she was uneasy around him, wary.

"That's Ahmed Abhoud, son of the Saudi ambassador, the former owner of my new limousine. Isn't it spectacular?"

"I'll say. Let's have a look."

They got out of the car and walked over to Mr. Pibb, who tipped his cap and smiled politely at them both, and Ahmed Abhoud, who clicked his heels, gave a little bow, and kissed them lightly on both cheeks.

"Luna, so good to see you, and who is your charming friend?"

Luna introduced Kat, who seemed to be quite taken with Ahmed.

"Well, then," he said, nodding at them both. "I was just explaining the features of the car to your Mr. Pibb."

"Please continue, then," said Luna.

Ahmed waved an arm at the limousine, with a flourish reminiscent of a game show model. "What you have here is the Rolls Royce edition of a 2013 BMW 550i, with a thirty-inch stretch over the ordinary 550i. Black, of course, nothing special about the exterior except the flag holders up front, but with heavy armor plating and bulletproof glass. Extras you probably will not need. Um, and heavy window tinting, of course, to keep those prying eyes of the press at bay." He winked at them.

Luna rolled her eyes and managed a wry smile. "Tell me about it."

Ahmed opened the passenger door. "The reason the limo is available is because it only seats two in the back. We have moved up to four-seaters. Still, I think you will like it."

"Can we get in?" asked Kat. Luna couldn't believe how openly Kat was flirting with him. She was almost fawning.

"Certainly," he said, waving them in. "Lower the window. Yes, that button there, and I will give you a tour of the interior features."

Luna and Kat climbed in, immediately sinking into the soft leather seats.

He appreciated their reaction. "All leather, of course, the finest. Both seats facing forward in separate cockpits, if you will." He started pointing from one feature to another. "Rear vanity mirrors, two electric ports for laptops, AM-FM-CD with controls up there, Bluetooth, GPS, USB ports, a TV facing each of you, of course, assist straps, coat hooks, LED reading lamps, center console bar with glassware and ice chest, the whole car fully insulated for temperature and sound, multiple A/C ports with boost fans, a roll-down privacy divider between you and Mr. Pibb, and a hands-free intercom system."

"And look," said Kat. "Cup holders."

Ahmed laughed. "You Americans and your cup holders. Yes, Miss Murphy, a ton of cup holders."

"Wow," said Luna. "This is far more than I was expecting, especially for the price. It even smells new."

He gave her a little nod. "I will always respond to a woman in need."

"Well, Ahmed, I truly appreciate this. I owe you one."

Ahmed beamed. "Perhaps we can talk about that sometime, *soon.*"

"Indeed, we shall." Luna grew quiet. She and Kat stared up at Ahmed, who was the first to blink.

"Okay, then, I will leave you and Mr. Pibb to it. Mr. Pibb has the documents you will need for registration." He tapped his hand on the window ledge, turned, and walked toward another limousine parked in front of hers.

Luna called after him. "Thank you so much, Ahmed."

He didn't say anything or even turn around. He just raised his hand and waved goodbye over his shoulder.

Mr. Pibb leaned in the window. "Shall we take 'er for a spin, ladies?

Kat almost squealed. "Yes!"

27

Parking Lot, British Geological Survey, Nottingham, Monday Morning, October 17.

Bruce sat in his car and tried to collect himself before entering the building. He had hoped to stop at his apartment to change into something more businesslike, but traffic had been bad. He would just have to accept that he would face Old Nozzle in his casual jeans, which made him uncomfortable. Old Nozzle was a stickler for rules.

He knew he'd be greeted by Old Nozzle the moment he stepped inside, and he wanted to be able to present a clear, logical, and defensible position on his decision to take the documents and shell fragments home. It was going to be a tough sell.

The drive from London had been uneventful. In fact, he had been in a zone most of the time, unaware that he was driving, thinking about last evening's discussions with Kat and Luna. Kat had been unable to take away the artist's sketch, but she was able to describe the dragon-man in great detail.

Luna had asked that he print out copies of the Darwin documents from his scans, but Bruce had vetoed the idea. The dragon-man seemed to have an appetite for the documents, even copies, so he didn't want them to push their luck. Instead, he used Luna's computer to send the documents to his computer at work, his home laptop, and when Kat insisted, to her laptop. They each would read the documents, Kat for the first time, and then compare notes by phone on Monday evening, which now seemed a long time away.

He wondered how Luna's morning was going. Despite all that was happening, despite her swollen hand — *what a fantastic punch!* — he knew she was still excited about taking delivery of her new limousine and her first day with Mr. Pibb. *Pontius. What parent would name their child Pontius?*

Before returning to Luna's apartment, they had celebrated the punch and the limo in Kat's apartment with a bottle of Duct Tape Chardonnay, which despite Kat's glowing recommendation, was abysmal. Not that anyone cared. They were just happy to be away from the press and the police interrogations. And Luna was happy to take the edge off her painful hand, which had bruised and swollen up quickly before they even had a chance to ice it.

Any thoughts of cleaning Luna's apartment were put aside for the night. In fact, Luna had already decided to call in a cleaning crew first thing. So they had just pulled the mattress back on the bed and drawn a sheet over themselves before falling fast asleep. When he awoke just before dawn, Luna was still purring away, so he had dressed quietly and headed for Nottingham.

Bruce could tell from the people walking past his car — the people who were invariably late on Monday mornings — that he should get moving. He zipped up his jacket and got out of the car. His cubicle buddy Gordon was on him at once.

"I say, old man, quite a weekend, eh?"

Bruce couldn't believe his luck. He could tell by Gordon's smile that he was eager to get inside and spend most the morning talking about Bruce, Luna, and the events of the weekend.

"Yes, quite a circus."

"Is it true then, all this monster talk?"

Bruce didn't answer. He pulled open the building door, nodded to the security guard, and walked as fast as he could to the elevator, the doors closing just before Gordon could jump on.

The other staff on the elevator backed away from him and followed strict elevator etiquette: no talking, no touching, look straight ahead or at the overhead floor numbers. Someone was putting out a force field of jasmine perfume. The doors opened and Bruce stepped out quickly and headed down the hall to his cubicle office. He could hear laughter behind him.

Old Nozzle was sitting in Bruce's chair, his arms folded against his chest, the small broken barrel in front of him on the desk, a security guard and a stack of empty boxes behind him.

"Well, well," Old Nozzle said to the guard. "Looks like our hero is here at last." He turned and looked up at Bruce, shaking his head in disgust at Bruce's jeans.

"Welcome back, Mr. Cargo, so glad you could join us this morning. Have a seat, won't you?"

28

Darwin's Study, Down House, Downe, 4:25 p.m., Monday, April 24, 1882.

Lily waited until Etty had closed the door and then immediately moved to the desk and sat down in Darwin's roller chair. She tried the lower left drawer of the desk, but it was just as she suspected: locked. She scanned the top of the desk for the key, but the room was too dark to make out the smaller objects.

She stood and moved to the curtains, opening them just a little, the afternoon light streaming in across the desk, dust motes dancing in the air. No key.

She began opening drawer after drawer, searching for the key. As she searched through the bottom right drawer, she heard the door open, the room growing even brighter.

"You won't find it there," said Emma.

Lily looked up to see Emma silhouetted in the doorway. She was wearing a mourning dress Lily knew well from memory. Emma had worn the same dress when her daughter Annie had died. It was black, of course, but far grander than the bombazine dresses worn by the masses. Hers was the more expensive choice: non-reflective Parramatta silk trimmed with crape, a hard, scratchy silk with a strange crimped look.

"Where might I find it, then?" Lily said.

Emma said nothing, but stormed into the room, past the desk, and closed the curtains with a firm tug. "And you opened the curtains. You know that is forbidden."

Lily sat back in the chair. "Superstition, nothing more."

Emma ignored the comment. "I told you that I didn't want to see you again, and yet here you are."

"I need his notebooks about me."

Emma huffed. "And you think I would give them to you? Do you have any idea how dangerous those notebooks are? If they were to be shown to the world, Charles would be a laughing stock."

"I don't plan to show them to anyone."

"But why do you need them?"

Lily sighed. "I'm hoping they contain notes about my brother as well."

"And why would you think that?"

"Charles said once that he had a theory about me and my brother, and I suspect his thoughts are in those notebooks."

"I'm sorry, but I just don't understand," said Emma, sitting down in the guest chair opposite Lily.

"He wondered what differences there would be between us. My brother was birthed live, and I hatched from an egg. He wondered which of us was more human.

"Well, wouldn't that be your brother?"

"On the face of it, yes, but Charles wasn't sure."

"Not sure?"

"He said he would have to observe and study my brother to be certain. As he did with me."

"Of course, but why is this so important to you?"

A shiver ran through Lily. "I saw him once, my brother, or thought I did, at that doomed performance at the Royal Pavilion. He was tall and muscular, and when his eyes locked on mine, I felt something—it's hard to describe—a power unlike I had ever felt. It was as if having him close made me stronger. So I wonder about that, and I also wonder about his intentions."

"Intentions?"

"Yes, as strong as I felt when I was near him, I also felt something else. Fear. Almost uncontrollable fear.

29

Briefing Room 3, Scotland Yard, Monday Morning, October 17.

The teams had received their marching orders and dispersed to do their assigned tasks, leaving DI Morton and Divers sitting at the front of the briefing room.

"Sir, you wanted to talk with me?" she said.

"Yes, I wanted to thank you personally for the fine briefing."

"Just doing my job, Harry."

"And I wanted to ask you about your gut feeling about this one."

She didn't know where he was going. "Sir? I'm not sure I know what you want me to say. My job is to collect facts and present them. It's not to speculate."

"But you have to wonder, don't you? All this nonsense about monsters and dragons, can it possibly be true? I mean, logic says we're dealing with a hoax, but I tell you, I completely believed everything that Murphy, Fearnow, and Cargo told me during questioning."

She nodded. "I see what you mean, Harry, but have you actually *read* those Darwin documents?"

"No, they're locked up in the evidence room for now. That's my next step, to read them and then get expert opinions about their authenticity and content."

"Perhaps that's where you'll find your answer, sir, in the complete concatenation of the facts."

He flashed a smile at her. "*Complete concatenation?* I like that, and perhaps you're right. But I'm going to press you nonetheless. What does your gut tell you, right now, at this minute?"

"I think Sherlock Holmes had it right, Harry. When you eliminate the impossible, what remains, however improbable, must be the truth. Or at least I think that's how it goes."

"So, what does your *current concatenation* tell you?"

She lowered her voice and leaned toward him. "That we're dealing with a bloody monster, Harry. And we best be right quick about finding it."

30

Thames Foyer, The Savoy, Strand, London, Monday morning, October 17.

Ahmed sat at a small table, enjoying coffee and a scone. He had insisted on a table that gave him a clear view of anyone's approach, and he was not disappointed when he saw the Tanzanian heading his way.

He lifted the silver coffee pot by way of greeting. "Darweshi, may I pour you a cup?"

Ahmed thought he'd never get used to the Tanzanian's stern, all-business look, complete with a menacing scar across his cheek, which now glowed silvery in the light coming from the large glass cupola above them, the signature feature of this amazing dining room. Dewji's muscles bulged under his suit jacket, which Ahmed could tell was at least a size too small. He would have expected a hit man to be more tailored. *Let it go.*

He took a deep breath and looked up at the cupola. All the light streaming in relaxed him, made him feel safe.

Darweshi Dewji looked left and right nervously, then sat down. "I told you we should meet in a private place, Ahmed, without so many people around."

In fact, the place was near full of wealthy people enjoying their breakfasts, silverware clinking almost musically, and thumbing through tourist guide books to plan their day.

"Have you never heard of hidden in plain sight?"

"I do not like this."

"Relax. A scone perhaps?" He lifted the plate of scones, the chocolate ones, his favorites. *Oh, the fragrance.*

Darweshi shook his head. "No, let's get on with it."

Ahmed wiped his mouth with a soft cloth napkin—how he loved these little luxuries—and sat back in his chair. "I have made the delivery."

"And the device and alterations?"

"Done and done." He pulled a mobile from his suit pocket and slid it across the table to Darweshi. "When you turn it on, you will be on a special GPS app that will track them."

Darweshi turned on the phone and a map appeared, indicating that the limousine was now in downtown London, not far from where they sat. "Good, and the switch?"

"There at the bottom, the red button. When you are ready to intercept them, just punch that and the engine will die. They will be sitting ducks."

"And the gas?"

"Triggered as soon as the kill switch goes active. Oh, and the doors will lock, so they will not be able to avoid the gas."

"And how do we unlock the doors?"

"When you click on the red button, a new screen will come up with a second button for unlocking the doors. Wait about thirty seconds, and you will be fine. They will be out for hours."

Darweshi smiled. "My benefactor will be very pleased."

Ahmed raised a finger. "One thing."

"Yes?"

"Perhaps you should wait until this publicity dies down. I mean, the press is on her case now."

Darweshi considered this, and shook his head. "No, we can do this now, in the next day or so. It would be natural for her to try to disappear for a while, to avoid the press."

"I guess that's true."

"And before the press is any wiser, or even her close friends and colleagues, we will have her, and my benefactor will have the magic he seeks. To have an albino of such renown—it can only enhance the magic."

Ahmed thought the use of albino blood and body parts in magic rituals was beyond barbaric, but he couldn't think about that now. What he had to think about was his own life and clearing the debt that would save him. Still, he had to ask.

"And the chauffeur?"

"A casualty. It will look like a heart attack."

So much blood, he thought, *but so much money.* "And the limo?"

"A new home for sea life. Not to worry."

"And your part of the deal, Darweshi?"

Darweshi smiled, which made his scar appear to writhe like a snake on his cheek. "Of course."

He pulled an envelope from his jacket and slid it across the table to Ahmed, who started to open it. Darweshi was quick to slap his hand firmly on top of Ahmed's. "Count it later."

Ahmed nodded. "Of course."

"It is exactly half, as agreed. I will leave you a coded message, as we agreed, on your mobile when it is done. We will meet the following morning at 9:00 for the final payment."

"Here?"

Darweshi looked around and grudgingly nodded. "Very well."

He lifted his hand, gave Ahmed a quick nod, and left, walking quickly out of the foyer. Ahmed picked up the envelope and slid it into his inner suit pocket.

He took a sip of his coffee. Cold.

31

In the Neighborhood of the Preston-Manfred Agency, London, Monday Morning, October 17.

Pibb had made a quick loop of the surrounding neighborhood to give Luna and Kat a chance to try out all the features of the limousine, while he was having the time of his life driving this new beast, which seemed extremely nimble for its weight.

The intercom interrupted his reverie. Luna's voice came on. Kat was giggling in the background. "Mr. Pibb, let's get back to the agency so Kat can be on her way."

He started looking for some sort of button to push so he could answer her, then remembered that the system was hands free. "Yes, madam."

Five minutes later they pulled up behind Kat's little car.

"Is that a genuine Mini, Ms. Murphy?" he asked.

"Yep, and it's a gas to drive," Kat shot back.

"I used to own one years ago. I still remember the speed thrill."

"Well, I'll have to give you a ride sometime."

Luna interrupted. "I warn you, Mr. Pibb. The speed thrill may be more than you bargained for. Kat has a lead foot."

Pibb laughed. "That little car right begs for speed, doesn't it, Ms. Murphy?"

"That's what I've been trying to tell Luna! And please, call me Kat."

"Well, then," said Luna, interrupting. "Time for Kat to be on her way. We're already running behind schedule, I'm afraid."

"Oh, all right," said Kat, opening the door and getting out. "Give me a ring when you're on your way home. I'll pull together a quick dinner for us."

Luna smiled at her. "That would be wonderful."

Kat gave her a little wave and closed the door. Luna hoped the new photographer would work out. Kat, at least, seemed to be taking it seriously, breaking from her style a bit with tailored black slacks and a matching long frock coat. The shoes were all Kat, though: sexy, open-heeled, black-suede sandals that seemed just right for her but all wrong for the weather. Seconds later, she was speeding away, perhaps overly fast, to impress Mr. Pibb.

"She's a bit of a bubble, if you don't mind my saying so," said Pibb.

"She is, she is. The exuberance of youth, if you will. And I absolutely adore her."

Pibb cleared his throat. "Ms. Fearnow, do you mind if I roll down this window between us. I feel like an astronaut communicating with home base."

Luna laughed. "Not at all, Mr. Pibb."

The window hardly made a sound. "There then," he said. "Where to, madam?"

"I don't have any shoots today—cancelled them—so the first stop will be at my dojo."

"Your what, madam?"

"A gym, Mr. Pibb, where I take lessons and practice a martial art called Wing Chun."

"Well, that certainly explains that punch of yours. I about laughed my—well, I mean, I thoroughly appreciated it, madam."

"Not my best effort, I'm afraid. I didn't follow through correctly, and I have the banged up hand to prove it."

"So this is like Kung Fu or something?"

"Sort of. It's a system developed by a woman named Yim Wing Chun. Very scientific, and it gives a smaller person the advantage in close, hand-to-hand fights. Given my vision, that's important. There are seven principles and techniques to master. I'll tell you about them along the way. It'll be good to talk about something other than what's been happening the past few days, and hopefully avoid the press."

"Our luck's held so far, miss. And as for all this publicity, perhaps you should consider your Abe Lincoln's Law."

Luna giggled despite herself. "Oh, Mr. Pibb, and which one of your many laws would that be?"

"When you have got an elephant by the hind legs and he is trying to run away, it is best to let him run."

"So you think this will all run away?"

"Oh, I know it seems oppressive, madam, but the press has a short attention span. Best let 'em run and be done with it."

"Well, I think we should do the running, at least for now."

She gave him the address, and she could hear him punching it into the GPS.

"Okay, madam, here we go."

32

Briefing Room 3, Scotland Yard, Monday Morning, October 17.

Harry sat in the front row of the empty briefing room, reflecting on the case, particularly the interview with Luna Fearnow.

He had been startled by her at first. He'd never had much experience dealing with people with albinism, and he knew she had sensed his discomfort. But his reaction had been nothing, apparently, in comparison to the reaction of Detective Sergeant Kafil "Bennie" Kadika, one of a half dozen officers of African origin on the team, and his partner for the interview. The big man—an imposing figure at six feet five—had taken a step back and stared intently at her, eyes wide.

"DI Morton," she had said, as calmly as can be, "would you please tell the gentleman behind you to stop staring at me like a cow stares at a new fence."

That had broken the ice, at least for him. It was another matter for Bennie, although he had done his best to recover and behave more professionally. "I am truly sorry, Ms. Fearnow. You startled me. In my birth country, people like you are rare."

"People like me?" she had said, leveling her gaze at him and shaking her head in disgust. "You mean *albinos* like me? Yes, and in some countries we're killed or abandoned at birth by our parents. Or we're hunted down for our body parts. Use my

blood or my hand in a ceremony and I'm suddenly big magic. You'll have good luck and wealth for the rest of your life. Oh, and while you're at it, rape me and I'll cure your AIDS!"

"Sorry," Bennie had said, "I didn't mean—"

She had interrupted, leveling her gaze at him. "Fine," she had said, turning back to Harry, then quickly back to Bennie. "And my name is pronounced Fear-NO, not Fear-NOW."

Harry had apologized to her and set about the interview, which was almost relaxing by comparison. By the end of the questioning, the fact that she had albinism had been replaced by a genuine interest in her as a woman. Her beauty. Her confidence. The way she spoke and moved. She was a handful, an absolute stunner, and he was at least under her spell, if not thoroughly besotted.

A door slammed behind him. Sergeant Tompkins was rushing toward him, a look of concern on his face.

"What's up, Fred?"

"That *thing*, sir! The evidence room. Come quick!"

33

Parking Lot, British Geological Survey, Nottingham, Monday Morning, October 17.

Bai Li, Sixth Assassin of the Red Dragon, drummed his long fingers on the dashboard of the black van. Huang Peng sat next to him, hands firmly gripping the steering wheel as he scanned the parking lot.

"Do you think he saw us?" said Huang Peng.

"Why should he?" Almost two hundred years later, and Huang Peng still didn't measure up. But the Inner Council would not listen to Li's pleas for a competent replacement. He and Peng were a team, they said, and there was no time now that the Green Dragon was due to awaken. *How could they be so sure, these old men? They'd said this before. And they'd been completely wrong about the white dragon, after all.*

Huang Peng didn't respond. He could tell from the tone of Li's voice that any response would lead to further rebuke. He had at least learned that much over the years. Then he spotted the man they were looking for. He was walking across the parking lot, carrying a cardboard box.

"There he is," said Peng.

Li glanced up quickly, grabbed the door handle and jumped out of the van. "Come!"

Peng jumped out of the driver's side and joined Li. They walked as quickly as possible across the lot, the man now almost at the door of the building.

"Mr. Doyle!" Li shouted.

The man stopped and turned, and gave them a menacing look. *Who were these people dressed all in black?*

Li raised a hand. "We are friends, Mr. Doyle, do not be afraid."

"Yes, friends," said Peng, which earned him a stern look from Li.

The man looked back and forth between them. "How do you know my name?"

Li bowed and Peng quickly followed suit. "My name is Bai Li and this is Huang Peng. We have been sent to help you on your quest, and we bring news of your father."

The man seemed to relax.

These men have albinism, too, Jamie thought. *I should at least hear them out.* If he didn't like what he heard, he could easily kill them.

"Call me Jamie."

34

Bruce's Cubicle, British Geological Survey, Nottingham, Monday Morning, October 17.

Old Nozzle had wanted to sack him on the spot, but Bruce persuaded him to hear him out. He had rambled on for some minutes, Old Nozzle sitting there, taking it all in but not relaxing his frown one bit. The guard seemed amused by the whole story and was having a hard time controlling himself.

"And that's the truth, all of it," Bruce said.

Old Nozzle continued frowning. "So you expect me to believe that the esteemed Charles Darwin was involved with dragons, that he wrote a secret journal and put it in a barrel with an egg, that he shipped it to someone who never received it, that it somehow magically appeared in our gloomy corner nearly two hundred years later, and that all this nonsense about the dragon-man is real and not some hoax you cooked up to discredit this institution?"

"Yes."

Old Nozzle shouted at him. "The press is *laughing* at us, Cargo. Laughing! Did you know that? Do you know how much you've damaged the Survey with this little *stunt* of yours?"

"Yes, I know they haven't been kind. But no, this is no stunt."

"Not kind?" he shouted. "They've all but destroyed us! My career is on the line."

Bruce had wondered how long it would take for everything to be about Old Nozzle. Not long, it seemed. He shook his head and raised his voice. "Yes, but what I'm saying is true nonetheless."

Old Nozzle took a deep breath, trying to calm himself. "Why are you so sure?"

"I've read the documents, I've seen what this dragon-man can do, and I think the police will confirm it all once they've analyzed the evidence."

"The police, yes. I'm meeting with a detective inspector later today to discuss just that. I've asked him to bring along these so-called documents and fragments, so we can have a look as well. Real or no, you should have *never* let them have any of it. It's all the property of the Survey, including those so-called egg fragments."

"I know that, but they didn't give me a choice. And I don't think bringing the documents and fragments to you is a good idea. The dragon-man seems to sense their presence, and comes for them."

Old Nozzle chuckled sardonically. "The dragon-man, indeed. Well, that's just *absurd*. Cryptozoological poppycock. He heaved a big sigh. "Cargo, I don't believe any of this, but I do think that in some demented, delusional way you actually believe what you've been telling me."

Bruce tried to control his anger. "I definitely do."

"And I maintain it's a *hoax*."

And then Bruce couldn't help himself. "Well, if it is, Flaps is behind it."

"Jamie? My god, man, now you're accusing a fellow scientist?"

"I'm just saying, if you're right, it certainly wasn't *me* who crafted what you call a hoax."

Old Nozzle turned to the guard. "You can go, but leave the boxes." The man nodded and left, giving Bruce a parting smirk.

"I had planned to can you this morning, Cargo, and still might, but I'll listen to what this detective inspector has to say before making any final decision. In the meantime, go home. You're too much of a distraction here."

"Yes, sir."

Old Nozzle pointed a finger at him. "And from this moment, you're officially on suspension without pay until I tell you otherwise."

Without pay rang in his ears as he left the cubicle, walked down the hall, and took a thankfully empty elevator down to the lobby and out the front door. He took a few steps and froze. About thirty yards away, Jamie was climbing into a black van with two men dressed in black. *The black van?*

35

Wing Chun Institute, Soho, London, Monday Afternoon, October 17.

The drive to Luna's dojo was uneventful, Luna going on and on about Wing Chun and its principles. Seemed very complicated to Pibb, certainly more so than boxing. The key elements seemed to be balance, yours and your opponents, controlling your opponent's elbow, fighting on his blind side, not fighting force with force, and using something called Chi Sao to sense what your opponent was likely to do next. All of it designed for close-in fights. Perfect for someone with albinism.

Frankly, Pibb couldn't wrap his head around it, so throughout the trip he mostly nodded his head and used "uh-huh" to indicate he was following her, which he definitely wasn't. Now that he was in the dojo and watching her perform, though, it was starting to make a little more sense.

There was no doubt that she had mastered it, as evidenced by the way she dispatched attackers one after another using just her one good hand. Her master had seemed pleased with her workout and had invited her to teach a class, which kept them at the dojo well past 2:00, much longer than either of them had planned.

She had eventually emerged from the locker room, back in her jeans and sweater again, sipping from a bottle of water, and beaming.

"That was amazing, madam, truly amazing."

"I told you, didn't I? You should really give it a try. I mean, we'll be coming here often, so why not pass the time with a class or two?"

Pibb wasn't sure how to respond to that. Since he had given up boxing, exercise was a lesser part of his life. Still, he could certainly do with the work on his paunch. "Indeed, madam. I shall give it some thought. Might be just the thing."

Luna sensed his reluctance. "Seriously, it could tone you up in no time. I'll even help with the fees, work a deal with the master."

Blimey, he thought, *I'll definitely have to ask her for an advance.* "Yes, madam, that would be wonderful." *Does she think I'm flabby?*

"All right, then, my teaching that class means we need to cross a few things off the list, do some quick grocery shopping at Sainsbury's, head on back to my apartment in Haggerston, and then call it a day."

"Yes, madam." *Haggerston? How will I get back home from there?* "Um, I'm not familiar with public transport from there. Do you know how I would get to Finsbury Park?"

"Oh," she said. "I guess I never made that clear. I was hoping you'd take the limo home with you each night and then pick me up at my apartment each morning. Would that be a problem?"

Pibb breathed a sigh of relief. "That would be perfect, madam. I have a friend named Jack who runs a repair shop near me. Gated and very secure. I'm sure he'd let me park the limo there every night."

"Sounds like a plan."

Pibb opened the back door of the limo for her, taking care not to knock off her fedora, and then closed it once she'd settled in.

He stepped to the front of the car, got in, and rolled down the window separating them.

"Are you sure you want to go to Sainsbury's, what with all the publicity and so forth?"

"Yes, I've decided to take Mr. Lincoln's advice — and yours — Mr. Pibb. Let the damn elephant run. If it runs at me, you've seen what I can do."

"Indeed, madam, indeed."

"So, Mr. Pibb, can I ask you a question about all this? The publicity. The stories. A dragon-man flying about."

Pibb shook his head. "I'm not sure my opinion counts for much, madam. All I know I learned from watching the telly, which means I know next to nothing."

Luna laughed. "I know what you mean, but come on, tell me what you think."

Pibb paused a moment. "All right. Firstly, I'm pretty much a romantic, so fantasy appeals to me. The possibility that there's something out there, some sort of dragon, actually excites me — except for the death by dismemberment part, of course."

"You are a man of many sides, Mr. Pibb. Tell me, are there any laws to guide us in this matter?"

"Madam, there are always laws. Let me think." He drummed his fingers on the steering wheel. "Of course, there are two, and they are both cautionary."

"Out with it."

"The first is Tolkien's Law: *It does not do to leave a live dragon out of your calculations, if you live near him.*"

"Ha! And the second?"

"That would be Bilbo's Law: *Never laugh at live dragons.*

36

Penthouse, The City Mills, Haggerston, Monday Afternoon, October 17.

Kat's morning shoot had gone extremely well, but as it had involved painting her entire body to resemble a silver robot, cleaning up had been a challenge. The second shower at home had done the trick for the most part. Just a few flecks of paint on what little pubic hair she had, and she could deal with those easily enough as she paced about the apartment toweling herself down.

After the shoot, she had gone straight to the archery range to try out her new bow and those new techniques on shooting the bow with the arrow on the right instead of the left. Her first attempts had been comical, but after an hour or so, she was getting a feel for how to quickly nock an arrow and fire it rapidly, even on the run. An hour after that and she was able to fire off three arrows at different targets in rapid succession, running as fast as she could. Well, once, anyway. More times than not, she fumbled with the second arrow and had to stop and start over again. But she could see progress, and couldn't wait to show Luna what she'd learned. It would be a good supplement to that martial art she practiced, Wing Something Or Other.

After her archery practice, she had stopped at the supermarket to get a few things for dinner, and the wine shop to pick up a case of Duct Tape Chardonnay. Luna and Bruce had thoroughly enjoyed it, so why not lay in a supply? Lugging it to the apartment had been a problem, but now two bottles were chilling in the fridge.

She saw the new bow leaning up against the couch, and picked it up, striking a pose. She'd have to mention this to tomorrow's photographer—Jason or Jack, she couldn't remember which. It would make a fantastic layout for *Sports Illustrated*, maybe even a swimsuit cover. *A girl can always dream.*

37

Evidence Room, Lower Level, Scotland Yard, Monday, October 17.

Just once, Harry would have liked to be ahead of the game when it came to dealing with the press, but this latest assault, which had left a gaping hole in the side of the building, was quickly filled with the reporters and cameras that had already been in place out front to cover the ongoing story.

With the help of Tompkins and three other officers, he'd managed to push the reporters fifty yards back up the alley, and cordon off the area. Fortunately, Divers had not yet left the building, so she was quickly on the scene.

"Well, Harry," she said after spending just a few minutes looking around. "At least no one was killed or injured."

Harry nodded. "Yes, there's that."

"Same method of entry—blunt force—this time through brick and concrete. Darwin evidence gone. A couple of white hairs to deal with. Hopefully, more and better video."

"Why is it so keen on those documents do you think?"

"Your guess is as good as mine. I just wish someone had read them before we lost them."

Harry hung his head. "And that should have been me reading them."

"Wasn't pointing, Harry. Just saying."

"I know. So, absent the documents and the fragments, we'll have to rely on Fearnow, Murphy, and Cargo. I'll have to call them back in."

"Yes, sir," she said. "If you don't need me, I'd best get back to it."

"Right, send me a copy of your report when you can. I'll be heading to Nottingham to join up with the local constabulary and talk to Cargo's superior." He sighed. "And try to explain how we managed to lose everything. A fun day ahead."

"Enjoy."

38

The Black Van, Monday, October 17.

Now that Jamie was in the van, he was clearly having second thoughts about his decision to go anywhere with these strangers. Making things worse, it had begun to rain, a driving rain that near turned the outside world invisible, the wipers not able to keep up, making him feel claustrophobic.

"Where are we going?" It was clear they were heading out of town, into the countryside.

The man at the wheel, Huang Peng, started to answer but was interrupted by the other man, Bai Li, who was sitting next to Jamie in the back seat. *This taller one is clearly the other's superior.*

"Many places," he said cryptically. "For now, we will drive around a bit, and talk."

In this rain? Jamie thought. "About what, may I ask?"

The man turned and smiled at him. "About you to begin with, and what you may or may not know about your destiny."

"Destiny? Why should I tell you anything?"

Bai Li nodded. "Fair enough. You should tell us everything we ask and be interested in what we have to say in return because we are your best hope of surviving the mistakes you have already made."

Jamie frowned. "Mistakes?"

"The apartment, the university, the dead professor, the evidence room at Scotland Yard, and the contents of that box you are holding so tightly. You have exposed yourself unnecessarily and soon forces will come into play to prevent you from doing what you *must* do. I know you have been isolated for many, many years, but believe me, you have enemies, many enemies, and now they know where you are."

"And what is it exactly that I must do?"

Li smiled at him. "Why, you must become the most powerful entity on the planet."

"I thought I already was that."

Huang Peng laughed out loud, causing Bai Li to admonish him with a quick slap the back of his head.

"Pay attention to the road!" Li shouted at him.

He turned back to Jamie.

"You are powerful, yes," said Bai Li, "but you can be killed, and there is another who is even more powerful, more powerful than you can even imagine."

"Who?"

"The proper question is *what*, and I think you already know, but we will get to that. First, I need you to answer a few questions. Can you at least agree to that?"

Jamie didn't know where this was going, but his curiosity was piqued. "All right."

Bai Li tapped Peng on the shoulder. "To the castle."

Jamie's eyes widened. "The castle?"

Bai Li smiled at him. "A long life may yield many rewards."

39

Police Car, On the Way to Nottingham, Monday Afternoon, October 17.

While Tompkins drove, Harry tried to call Luna and Kat, but both their mobiles were apparently off. Not surprising given the nature of the calls they'd probably be receiving from the press and other dotty fools. He was about to punch in Cargo's number, when his mobile rang.

"Morton here."

"Hello, inspector, it's Bruce Cargo." He had just guided his car to the side of the road so he could talk more freely with DI Morton without running off the road. He was only a few blocks from Luna's, and probably could have just continued on, but the memory of his crash while texting last year made him extra cautious when it came to cell phones and driving.

Harry smiled. "What luck, I was just trying to reach you."

"Oh?"

"Yes, I don't know if you've been watching the news, but the dragon-man has struck again."

"Wow, where?"

"Scotland Yard, I'm afraid, and it took the documents and fragments. Press is in a frenzy, of course."

"Shit!" Old Nozzle was going to "love" this.

"Exactly. It broke into the evidence room and took the entire box of stuff with it."

"God, I hope no one was—"

"No, no, everyone is fine, but it got away clean. So I was trying to reach you to see whether the four of us could get together for a chat tonight to discuss the documents and what they said. You're the only ones who've read them, so. . ."

"Of course, but you should know I managed to save computer copies of the documents."

Suddenly the day seemed brighter. "Whew, that's terrific!"

"I'll sit you down in front of Luna's computer tonight, and you can read them yourself."

"Or you could just e-mail them to me."

"No, I think it would be good for us to discuss them with you once you've read them. Not everything may make sense to you."

"All right, great. I'm on the way to your office to see Dr. Shepherd. Will you be around?"

Bruce sighed. "No, actually, I have, um, the day off. I'm back in London."

"Okay, then, I'll see you this evening, probably after 8:00 if that's okay."

"Yes, that will be fine."

"Later, then."

Bruce started to ring off, but the image of Jamie climbing into that black van came back to him. "Wait a second, I just thought of something. What do your evidence boxes look like?"

40

Darwin's Study, Down House, Downe, 4:35 p.m., Monday, April 24, 1882.

Lily could tell Emma was struggling with what best to do. "All right, you don't have to *give* me the notebooks. Just let me sit here in the study and read them. That's all I ask."

Emma sighed, then nodded. "Very well." She pulled the key from a handkerchief she had been clutching. "I'll give you the rest of the day. You can even open the curtains after I leave the room."

Lily smiled at her and took the key. "Thank you, Emma. It means a lot to me."

She leaned down to the drawer, inserted the key, and gave it a twist, the drawer clicking open. "There."

She pulled out the drawer, and her eyes went wide. "It's empty."

Emma blinked. "Empty? That's impossible." She stood and walked around the desk to look for herself. "I just don't understand this. He was so protective of them."

Lily slumped back in the roller chair. "I was so hoping."

"I know," said Emma. "I'm sorry. Truly, I am. I just don't know what to say."

"Did he have other hiding places?"

Emma looked around the room. "Not really. He would sometimes hide gifts behind books on the shelves, but his work, no, he would have locked that up. And this drawer is the only lockable place in the house."

"What about on the grounds?"

"What, do you think he buried the notebooks? That's ridiculous. He'd never do that."

"No, but I'm thinking the worst."

"The worst?"

"That he may have destroyed them. Burned them in the hearth."

Emma shook her head. "He would never destroy his work, even work that could destroy his reputation. He was just prideful that way."

Lily shook her head and stood. "There is nothing more I can do here. I will pay my respects to him and be on my way. And you needn't worry about me coming back. I know I am no longer welcome here."

Emma nodded and moved toward the door. Lily followed her out of the study and down the hall to the parlor, where Darwin's casket rested on two sawhorses. It was a large casket, rough-hewn from what looked like oak. It had bronze handles along the sides and ends for the pallbearers, and a brass plate inscribed with Darwin's name and the dates of his birth and death.

"How could there be a coffin so soon?" said Lily.

Emma nodded. "Do you remember young John Lewis, the carpenter's son?"

Lily smiled at the memory. "We had such fun playing with him. He was just a teenager."

"And now he is forty-eight and a bespoke carpenter in his own right. Charles had told him what he wanted some weeks ago, so John knew what to make."

"The casket does not seem grand enough for him," said Lily.

Emma smiled. "It was his decision. John said Charles wanted it rough, just as it left the bench, with no polish."

"Where will he be laid to rest?"

Emma huffed. "I thought by the local church here in Downe. Three of my children rest there, along with Charles's brother, dead these seven months."

"That sounds wonderful. I remember him talking about the old yew tree there. No, there can be no better resting place."

Emma sighed. "I agree, but now several of his colleagues have lobbied Westminster Abby for his interment there."

"Oh, I see. That would be quite an honor. Newton is buried there, is he not?"

"Yes, yes, but I tell you, that would never have been his wish."

Lily nodded and looked down at the casket once more. "Well, then, I will be on my way." She kissed her fingers and touched them to the casket. "My dear Charles."

Emma said nothing, stepping aside to make room for Lily to exit. "Take care, my dear."

Lily moved past her, walked down the hall and out through the front door. Emma followed at a distance and quickly shut and locked the door.

Lily shook her head at the sound of the lock, then turned and walked down the path to the road, where her carriage waited.

As she neared the carriage, she caught sight of Etty, beckoning her from the corner of the house. Lily turned back and walked across the lawn.

"What is it, Etty?"

"About the notebooks," she whispered.

"Yes?"

"She lied to you."

"What?"

"Lied, and I just can't abide it. The notebooks are in father's casket, hidden under his waistcoat."

Lily's eyes went wide.

"I know," said Etty. "She shouldn't have lied, but father was determined to take those notebooks to his grave."

Lily sighed. "Well, then, can you get them for me?"

Etty shook her head. "No, no, mother is sitting with him now, and will be until late in the evening. You must wait until well after dark. I will put a candle in the study window when it is safe for you to come in."

Lily nodded. "Very well, and thank you, Etty. I will not forget you for doing this for me."

Etty looked left and right. "I better go. I will be missed."

She said nothing more, but turned and fled down the length of the house to the back door.

41

The City Mills, Haggerston, Apartment 132.

Luna had had a great time with Mr. Pibb at Sainsbury's, although the fluorescent lighting had given her fits, as usual. Fortunately, she had all but memorized where things were in this particular Sainsbury, so finding things had not been as problematic as they would have been in an unfamiliar store.

She had picked up what she needed and he had done the same, thanks to the advance she had given him. *A cat's got to eat, after all.*

They had spent almost an hour there, Luna wandering off to pick up her items, Pibb doing the same to get his. He hadn't wanted to do a full shopping, but he did have a mind to get what he'd need for a good breakfast fry-up: eggs, bacon, sausages, black pudding, baked beans, bread, mushrooms, tomatoes, and a good coffee, a dark roast to get him perking, along with cat treats and a dozen tins of cat food.

From time to time, they would pass each other in the aisles, and by watching the people around her, he could see what she had to deal with every day of her life. The stares, the curiosity, the pointing, the laughter, the whispers, all manner of inappropriate behavior. He had a mind to slap some of them silly, but he knew that would just draw more attention to her, and that was something she did not need. And he was in awe of the way she handled herself: standing tall, confident, making *them* look away with the merest of glances. She was rapidly becoming a hero to him.

When they had finally met up at checkout, Luna had given him a surprised look when they compared shopping carts. She just had some French bread, a wedge of brie, a jar of raspberry jam, and six containers of Greek yoghurt, which he suspected was her go-to lunch.

The drive to her apartment had been pleasant enough, but when her building came in sight, they had both groaned. Fortunately, the press weren't expecting a limo, so they were able to quickly get inside before the cameras turned their way. No doubt the evening news would feature a shot of the two of them, Pibb laden with groceries, racing for the elevator.

Mr. Pibb had thought it was great fun, in a strange way — he had never been pursued by the press, not even when he was boxing professionally — but she was just thankful that she didn't have to throw another punch. When she opened the door to the apartment, he had whistled in awe at the destruction that, despite the efforts of the cleanup crew, was still apparent.

"Would you like something to drink, Mr. Pibb?"

Pibb shook his head. "No, madam. I best be on my way. Lucifer will be expecting me."

Luna giggled. "A cat's gotta eat."

"Yes, madam, and thank you again for the advance. It means the world to me, and to Lucifer, of course." He looked at the shopping bag he'd placed on the counter. "Can I help you put away the groceries?"

"No, that won't be necessary. You run along. And say hello to Lucifer for me."

"I'll do that, miss. So, what time tomorrow, then?"

Luna fumbled in her purse and pulled out her calendar. "Let me see now. Yes, I have a shoot at 10:00, so let's say you pick me up here at 9:30."

"Right, I'll ring you up when I arrive, so you can make a right dash for the car."

"Perfect."

42

Boorwick Castle, Ten Miles East of Bedford, Monday Afternoon, October 17.

Jamie watched the tall steel gate in the high stone wall swing open automatically as they approached, then swing closed as they drove on down a tree-lined drive to a massive castle, complete with towers and turrets.

"Impressive," he said.

Bai Li gave him a satisfied look. "If time has to pass, why not in luxury."

"You own this?"

"For well over a hundred years."

Jamie nodded knowingly. "So you are a guardian, like my father."

Bai Li shook his head. "Not exactly."

Jamie gave him a puzzled look.

"How should I put this," said Bai Li. "I do not want you to jump to the wrong conclusion when I tell you what I do."

"Why would I do that?"

"No reason, once you know that the *talents* indicated by my title would never be directed at you."

"And what title would that be if not Guardian?"

"I am the Sixth Assassin of the Red Dragon."

Jamie, taken aback, edged away from Bai Li. "Assassin?"

"As I said, not directed at you. My job, in fact, is to kill anyone who prevents you from completing the plan."

"The plan?"

Bai Li sighed. "Let us go inside. I am sure we both have many questions."

43

The Gladstone, Number 6, Finsbury Park, Monday Evening, October 17.

Pibb was huffing and puffing by the time he pushed open the door and set the groceries on the counter, Lucifer hopping up in full purr to see what treats might await.

"Give me a moment, Luci." He looked into one of the bags, dug down, and found and opened the box of cat treats.

"Here you go, boy. And there's more where that came from, thanks to my new employer. Perhaps one day you'll meet her. A lovely, lovely woman."

He picked up Lucifer, scratched him under the chin, and set him down on the floor. "Now, leave me alone a bit so I can empty these bags."

The drive from Haggerston to Finsbury Park had not been bad at all, even with the light rain that fell on and off, the GPS providing flawless instructions, although he felt the woman's voice on the bloody thing was a bit grating, particularly when he made a wrong turn. "Recalculating," she would say, with a snide tone to her voice. It could have been his imagination, but he was sure her voice grew more and more snide with each mistake he made.

He'd taken the limo directly to Jack, who was delighted by the apparent condition of the car and, more so, the chance to dig in and give her a good onceover. Pibb had taken out the groceries and walked the two blocks to his flat. Maybe Luna was right. He really was out of shape. His legs and arms were still burning from the effort.

He put the last tin of cat food away, grabbed a beer, and slumped down on the sofa. The number of reporters outside Luna's apartment building had given him pause. Their numbers seemed to be increasing, not decreasing. He grabbed the flipper and turned on the telly.

He didn't have to wait long. The first channel he tried was showing footage of a massive hole in the side of a familiar looking building. *Is that Scotland Yard?*

He turned up the sound, and listened to the reporter describe the scene. She seemed a bit too perky and smiley for the seriousness of the situation. *Ah, youth.*

"Here, just fifty meters from where I stand, is the site of the latest devastation credited to the dragon-man." *Oh, dear, she's smiling again.*

"A hole big enough for a lorry to drive through, punched right through brick and concrete, as if the building had been nothing more than a sponge cake." *Stop smiling!*

"Police throughout London and the countryside are now on full alert as the search for this powerful and strange creature continues." *Does she know her hair's a right mess? And that dress? Bad choice!*

She suddenly put on her serious frown look. "And now, in developing news, police have released a picture of what they call a *person of interest* in the case. His name is Jamie Doyle, an employee of the British Geological Survey, and he lives in the Nottingham area. If you know this man, or if you *are* this man, please contact the police immediately. You are not a suspect in the case, but police think you may have information that would help."

The telly cut to a photograph of a serious looking man, a large, muscular man with albinism. He looked a bit Chinese or Polynesian. The camera flash had made his eyes bright red. And then there was the reporter again and that irritating smile.

"This is Claire St. Clair reporting. Back to you Charles."

The television showed a close-up of Charles Nixby, the always insufferable anchor, who was shuffling papers in front of him. "Thank you, Claire, for that *insightful* reporting," he said with a smirk.

Then he turned and looked into another camera. "How long will it be before this menace, this terror, is apprehended and dealt with? That is the question on every Londoner's mind tonight."

He turned and looked at another camera. "And with that in mind, I'd like to turn to the gentleman next to me, Dr. Farley McKnight of the Cryptozoological Institute. Did I pronounce that correctly, doctor?"

The guest, a man in his forties with an almost clown-like ring of ginger hair around his otherwise bald head, nodded vigorously. "Indeed, you did, sir."

"Doctor, the more we get into this story, as insane as it seems, the more likely it is that we are actually dealing with a monster of some sort. As I understand it, your institute investigates such sightings."

The doctor gave a slight shake of his head. "Not exactly, Charles. We catalog the sightings. Our goal is to maintain a record of the sightings to aid in investigations and subsequent sightings."

"I see. Now, just how common are sightings like this?"

"Oh, my, they are actually more common than you realize. Our catalog includes more than four hundred separate cryptozoological beasts that have been sighted here in England. Some go back centuries, others are quite recent."

"Really?"

"Yes, there was an incident right here in London in 1844, for example. A child said to have a lizard-like body was exhibited at the Royal Pavilion Theater."

"You don't say?"

"Oh, yes."

"Interesting. So, anything more recent?"

"Indeed, aside from the sightings we are dealing with now, two fairly recent sightings of flying creatures come to mind. In 1982, for example, several witnesses reported seeing what looked like a pterodactyl flying over Yorkshire. There are even photographs, and it clearly was not a bird."

"A kite, perhaps?"

McKnight frowned. "As I said, we don't investigate. We just catalog and report."

"Hmm, well, 1982 is not all that recent. Anything in the past ten to twenty years, say?"

"Yes, a similar sighting of a pterosaur-like creature in January 2016, in Nursery Woods. No photographs of that one, but more than 200 people reported seeing it."

"But nothing like this dragon-man thing?"

McKnight shook his head. "Not this particular combination of features, although there are quite a few creatures in our database that have features common to man and other animals."

"You mean like Bigfoot and such."

"Yes, or creature's part man and part wolf, or part man and part snake, that kind of thing."

"Thank you, doctor, this has all been very interesting."

The camera zoomed in on the anchor, the guest disappearing from view. "And now I'd like to switch to a related story, the tragic death of a young man in a wingsuit who was performing a copycat stunt to mimic the dragon-man. That stunt failed when he lost control during his descent from one of the highest buildings in London."

The telly switched to a street scene. A body was draped with a blanket as policemen stood around.

Pibb turned off the telly. "The things people do, Luci. Boggles the mind, it does."

His mobile rang. "Pibb here."

It was Jack, and he seemed very excited, but not in a good way. "Get 'round here quick, Ponty. I've found something wrong with the car, and it's a complete bollocks."

"What, already? Can't it wait till morning? I'm getting ready to fix myself a bite and settle in to watch "Godzilla" on the telly."

"No, Ponty, you'll want to see this."

"See what?"

"I'd rather not talk on the phone about it. Can you come?"

Not talk on the phone? "Yes, I'll be right there."

Pibb grabbed a jacket and headed for the door, Lucifer padding along behind him.

"This is a variation on Campbell's Law, Luci: *The telephone never rings until you are settled in the water closet.*"

He leaned down and ran his hand along Lucifer's back. "Be right back, Luci, there's a good boy." His stomach growled.

44

Boorwick Castle, Ten Miles East of Bedford, Monday Evening, October 17.

As impressive as the castle had been from the outside, the inside was even more so. It was as if they had been transported back in time. Huge paintings and tapestries of long-dead men and women in eighteenth-century clothes, all looking far too serious, lined the walls; lavish oriental carpets on polished stone floors; every window a rainbow of stained glass, depicting dragons and knights and battle scenes; period furniture begging not to be sat upon; huge crystal chandeliers twinkling above them, casting strange shadows as they passed under them.

Bai Li and Huang Peng led Jamie through what must have served as a dining room—for thirty guests!—and into a room lined with computers and monitors. The latest news from every channel was being streamed on several large screens. An old photograph of Jamie was being broadcast on most of them.

"You see how popular you have become by your errant ways?" said Bai Li, motioning Jamie to sit at a small conference table at the center of the room.

"Peng, bring up the view of his building." Peng went to a keyboard and made a few keystrokes. One of the monitors blinked out, then came back with an image of several police cars, lights flashing, outside a residential building.

Jamie couldn't believe what he was seeing. "That's my building. How did you know this was going to happen?"

Bai Li tilted his head to one side. "My dear boy, we have been monitoring you for *years*. Not in such a fancy way at the beginning, of course. No computers back in 1834."

"And yet you never made contact with me in all those years."

"No, there was no reason. Our orders were to find you, monitor you, keep you safe, and contact you only when absolutely necessary."

"Like now?"

"Yes, you have been a rather reckless boy." He turned to Peng. "See if you can find us something to eat. And coffee."

Peng gave him an unhappy, sullen look, and left the room.

"I take it he's your assistant," said Jamie.

"Well, he tries." He watched Peng leave the room. "Somewhat."

"And your interest in me?"

"As I said, we are here to protect you so that you can complete your mission."

"And what would that be?"

"It is rather complicated. When you took it upon yourself to kill the white dragon and partake of its flesh, you became more than just stronger."

Jamie's eyes grew wide. "How did you know I became stronger?"

"It is a given, and key to the mission. When a dragon kills and consumes another dragon, it takes on that dragon's special powers, whatever they might be. For example, if a white dragon eats a green dragon, it will have the powers of both a white dragon and a green dragon. If it then goes on to kill and eat, say, a blue dragon, it will have those powers as well. Each kill makes it more and more powerful."

"But I am no dragon."

"Admittedly, not a full dragon, but you have the blood of a white dragon coursing through your veins, and a little red dragon as well. Admit it, when you ate the white dragon's blood and flesh, you did in fact become ten times more powerful."

Jamie nodded. "At least. It was as if I could not get enough of its flesh. The more I ate, the stronger I became. My muscles knotted, my vision became perfect, and I could fly higher, faster, and longer than I had ever done. I think my father hated me for it, because he could not prevent me from leaving."

Li let Jamie's comment about his father pass. "And you had the irresistible urge to be here in England."

"Yes, but I don't know why."

Peng came back into the room, carrying a tray of biscuits and coffee.

"Thank you, Peng." He nodded to Jamie. "I would offer you tea, as is the custom here, but we already know you detest it, that you prefer coffee. In fact, that you prefer this brand of coffee and can barely resist shortbread biscuits."

Peng poured a cup of coffee, adding one package of sweetener and a generous splash of cream, and handed the cup to Jamie.

"You seem to know everything about me." He took the cup and set it down in front of him, next to the box he'd carried in from the van.

"Certainly, after nearly two hundred years, I should hope so." He paused and tapped a finger on the table. "And yet, we do not know everything. That box you brought with you, for example. It must be very important to go to all this trouble."

Jamie looked down at the box. He was pleased he knew something they did not seem to know. "Documents, a letter and a journal, written by Charles Darwin."

Bai Li seemed puzzled. "Oh, on what subject?"

"On his meeting with my father, and the egg my father gave him to transport to England."

"Egg? What kind of egg?"

"The egg that once contained my brother. Nothing but fragments now."

Bai Li seemed stunned. "Brother?" *Why had the Inner Council not mentioned this?*

Jamie opened the box and pulled out the documents and a few of the egg fragments. "Yes, my brother."

Bai Li's eyes grew wide. He picked up a fragment and sniffed it. *Long since hatched.* "I should like to read those documents if you do not mind."

"Of course," Jamie said, pushing the documents across the table. "But first, you said you had news of my father."

Bai Li sat back in his chair and sighed.

PART THREE

And now, as we revel in the glorious reign of Zhu Houzhao, the Zhengde Emperor, the Red Dragon and his pale guardians have become but myth, stories to tell in the emperor's pleasure palaces, the Bao Fang, outside the Forbidden City, when the flesh is sated, drink is plentiful, and a fanciful tale told well in the emperor's "leopard chamber" is like an elixir for the soul. Some stories provoke laughter, others provoke tears, but stories of the Red Dragon, when they arise and the emperor nods his approval to begin, bring fear, prompting whispers among some that the Red Dragon sleeps but will awake one day to claim the throne for itself, ending the rule of man for all time. It is at these times when the emperor laughs the loudest. Still . . .

— Zhang Wei, *The Emperor's Dragons* (1513)

45

Jack's Lorry and Limo, Finsbury Park, Monday Evening, October 17.

The walk back to Jack's had taken Pibb considerably longer than his walk earlier in the evening, his legs burning from the effort. He caught sight of Jack from a block away, and he could see Jack swinging his arms at him, urging him to hurry up, but he was pretty much down to his last huff and puff.

"Coming!" he shouted, although his legs balked at a faster pace. When Jack finally unlocked the metal gate for him, Pibb had to bend over at the waist to catch his breath.

"Blimey, Ponty, are you *that* out of shape?"

"Apparently."

"Comes from sitting on your arse all day, it does. Too much driving, too much telly."

Pibb took a few more deep breaths and straightened himself. "Yes, I seem to be a victim of Smith's Fourth Law of Inertia: *a body at rest tends to watch the telly.*"

Pibb did not get the laugh he was hoping for, or the empathy. "Now, what kind of bollocks have you found?"

Jack started walking toward the shop. "Come along and have a look. I was no more than twenty minutes into my inspection, when I came upon a bloody scary thing."

He led Pibb into the shop, which smelled of diesel and gasoline. Everything glowed with strange colors under the fluorescent lights. The driver's door to the limo was open.

"So I was checking the lamps and such," said Jack, "when I noticed a wire out of place under the fascia. See?"

Pibb leaned into the car and bent over. A yellow wire was hanging down a few inches. "You brought me all the way back here for a wire?"

Pibb started to touch the wire, but Jack grabbed his hand. "I wouldn't do that, mate, might trigger something."

"Trigger?"

"I must admit, I almost touched it myself, then thought better of it. Fetched a torch and a mirror and slid in under there on my back. A couple of things going on."

"Yes?"

"Firstly, it's rigged with a kill switch."

"To stop the car or prevent it from being started. An anti-theft device, do you think?"

"No, the kill switch is just the beginning. There are wires leading to the door locks, to lock you in, and here's the scary part—there's a whole nest of wires leading to what looks like a couple of gas canisters, or maybe bombs."

"The bloody hell!"

"In a nutshell."

Pibb ran a hand through his hair. "And how would they trigger it, do you think?"

"Oh, that's clear enough. The whole thing is hooked to a mobile and a couple of other odd bits. They'd just ring it up and—BOOM!"

46

The City Mills, Haggerston, Apartment 132, Monday Evening, October 17.

Bruce, Luna, and Kat sat on the sofa, silently passing a large bowl of popcorn back and forth between them. Three wine glasses sat in front of them on the coffee table, two completely full, one nearly empty.

Detective Inspector Morton had arrived half an hour earlier, interrupting Luna's scolding of Bruce for being "such a wimp" in his meeting with Old Nozzle. She was pissed that he hadn't been more forceful in defending himself.

"Grow a pair, Bruce," she had screamed at him, and been immediately sorry for saying it. He had only time to say "you don't understand" before the doorbell rang and DI Morton presented himself.

Kat had arrived almost immediately after that, seemingly dressed for a party, two chilled bottles of Duct Tape Chardonnay in hand, so their argument had come to an abrupt and unsatisfying end. Luna had mouthed "I'm sorry" to him and he had nodded and offered a weak smile, but they would definitely have to have another talk before the end of the day.

DI Morton had come directly from his meeting with Old Nozzle at the Survey, and he gave them a quick rundown on the case, briefly discussing the search for Jamie — not a trace of him so far — and the progress of the investigation — still no DNA results on the break-in or the murder, but they had collected additional evidence from Jamie's flat and his office at the Survey. They felt confident that they could run him to ground forthwith.

Morton had also calmed down Bruce somewhat with news that Old Nozzle was finally coming around to accept that a monster of some kind was, in fact, on the loose, and that Bruce had had the good sense to save computer copies of the documents.

"He wants you back at work tomorrow," Morton had said.

"Well, that's good," Luna had said, giving Bruce a conciliatory look.

Luna had shown Morton to her office and set him up at the computer to read the documents. And while he did that, the three of them decided to do something as mindless as possible, which was to watch "Godzilla," the latest American version, which none of them liked.

If Luna had liked it even a little bit, she would have been sitting on the floor close to the screen, so she could actually see what was going on. Instead, she sat with the others on the couch, letting the movie's soundtrack guide her through the fuzzy images.

"This is stupid," said Kat just ten minutes into the movie. "Can we watch something else?"

"There's not much else on," said Luna. "The special effects are okay, but I much prefer the Matthew Broderick version. At least that one had some humor to it. This is just awful."

"Agreed," said Bruce. "You know the version I like the best? One of the early Japanese versions. I think it was the first, in fact."

"Those are kind of hokey," said Kat. "You can tell that Godzilla is just some guy in a rubber suit, crushing matchbox cars and balsa and papier-mâché buildings."

Luna laughed. "And all those Godzilla versus Mothra movies. Too funny. Remember those tiny singing princesses?"

They all laughed.

"So, anyway," Bruce continued. "There's this scene in the movie that just cracks me up every time. Godzilla is on a rampage in Tokyo, knocking over building after building. Meanwhile, a newspaper editor is watching the destruction from his high office window. It looks like the newspaper building is the only building left standing. I mean there is literally nothing left of Tokyo except this one building. Anyway, the phone rings in the editor's office. So he picks it up. It's a government official in some other city wanting to know what the situation is. And this is where it cracks me up. The editor looks out the window. Godzilla is stomping on what's left of Tokyo and swatting the last plane-on-a-string from the sky. And then the editor, in probably the greatest example of understatement ever recorded on film, picks up the phone and says—"

"*The situation is grim*," said Morton, walking into the room. "I love that movie!"

47

Boorwick Castle, Ten Miles East of Bedford, Monday Evening, October 17.

Bai Li had put off telling Jamie about his father, requesting that he first be allowed to read the documents. Jamie had agreed, reluctantly — *perhaps he had already guessed* — and Bai Li had set about reading.

Now, an hour later, he pushed the Darwin journal away from him and sat back in his chair. Zhao Yu, the guardian of the White Dragon, had told a convincing tale, if not altogether true. Most important, he had not revealed the Inner Council's true intentions in regard to the Red Dragon. That was good. On the other hand, he had told Darwin that the egg was not viable. Why the lie?

He turned to Jamie. "Have you read this?"

Jamie nodded. "Of course. I hoped to find clues that would lead me to my brother."

"To kill him?"

"No, of course not."

Li blinked at his answer, but let it pass. "Were you not able to sense him? Dragons are able to do that."

Jamie sighed. "At times I thought I did, but with two exceptions, there was always nothing."

"Exceptions?"

Jamie pointed at the documents and the shell fragments. "When I found those, in a small cask, for one. It's still at the office."

"Tell me about that. Did you smell it—white dragons have a keen sense of smell—or was it something else?"

"There was a scent, yes, but more than anything else, an intuition, a feeling that my twin was nearby."

"Where did you find this cask?"

"Strangely, it was under a tree, not far outside Liverpool, which is where I lived back then."

"Then?"

"Yes, the year 1834. I'd been there about seven years. Anyway, I had awakened from a dream and there was this compelling scent in the air. I just followed it from the docks for a few miles, and there was this cask. The ground was matted down around it, as if someone had slept alongside it, and there was a strong smell of rum and sweat that just ruined the scent."

"You could have followed the scent of rum, could you not?"

"No, it was strong around the tree, a lot had apparently been spilled, but three steps away from that tree and the scent disappeared in the wind. I tried walking in what I thought was a logical direction, but that proved wrong."

Bai Li drummed his fingers on the table. "A pity."

Jamie nodded. "Yes."

"And the second exception?"

"Even stranger. It was about ten years later, give or take. I was walking down a street in London one night, and I thought I heard a shriek much like mine when I'm, um, aroused."

"You saw nothing, smelled nothing?"

"No, and it was over very quickly, making me wonder whether I had even heard it. Wishful hearing, if you will."

"And nothing more? Not a single other time over all these many years?"

"For my brother, no. But there was another time, at a London theatre, when I saw a little girl transform. I didn't know what to make of it, someone like myself. I tried to find her, but she escaped."

"We know."

"What?"

"We were there, watching you watching her. Following you following her. And too bad for you; she was your sister. Is your sister. You do not have a brother, in fact. *She* is the one who emerged from the egg."

Jamie was stunned. "But—"

Bai Li held up a hand, then pointed to the journal. "In the documents, you are referred to as Zhao Jiao-long. Do you know what that means?"

"No, I have no idea."

"Jiao-long means *looks like a dragon.*"

Jamie shrugged. "So?"

"And your sister's name, Ju-long?"

He shook his head. "Really, I have no idea."

"It means *powerful as a dragon.*"

Jamie seemed puzzled. "And?"

Bai Li smiled wryly. "Given that, are you sure you want to meet your sister?"

"What, you think she would mean me harm?"

Huang Peng, who had been sitting quietly until now, slapped his hand on the table and laughed. "Of course. There can be only one."

Bai Li gave him a withering look. "You will remain silent!"

Huang Peng looked away. "As you wish."

Bai Li shook his head. "Forgive my apprentice. He is prone to these unfortunate outbursts." He gave Peng another angry look and turned back to Jamie. "To continue, what I worry about is how Zhao Yu named you. You were a live birth, which is more humanlike. Ju-long, on the other hand, hatched from an egg, more dragon-like. Your name says you *look* like a dragon; hers, that she is as *powerful* as a dragon. Does that not give you pause?"

Jamie shrugged, not sure what to make of it. "I guess."

"As it should. On the other hand, having killed the White Dragon, you may be the stronger. We shall see."

Bai Li picked up the journal and then dropped it back on the table. "Now, back to the documents."

"Yes?" said Jamie.

The documents clearly set out what is expected of you. Did you miss that?"

Jamie turned his hands palm up. "Apparently."

"As my apprentice said, there can be only one, much like that horrible Highlander series of movies. To put it simply, you have killed the White Dragon, and if you think back on it, you would agree that you had no real choice in the matter. You had to do it. You were compelled to do it. *Now* you must kill the Green Dragon and the other dragons, so you will be strong enough to fight and kill the Red Dragon."

"And I would want to do that because . . . ?"

Bai Li smiled. "Why, to become truly immortal, invulnerable, powerful beyond measure. You would be a god."

Jamie shook his head. "Suppose I say no?"

Bai Li threw back his head and laughed. "As I have said, you will not be able to resist. Once the Green Dragon hatches, you will feel compelled to find it and kill it."

Jamie slumped back in his chair. "And if my sister appears?"

Bai Li tilted his head to one side. "Why, you will kill her, too." He paused and then added, "Or she will kill *you.*"

"There can be only one?"

Bai Li nodded. "Indeed."

48

Outside Down House, Downe, 11:35 p.m., Monday, April 24, 1882.

Lily shuddered from the cold. She had been standing in a small grove of trees for two hours now, far enough away from the house to avoid detection and close enough to see the candle, when and if it ever appeared.

She had forgotten how cold it could get on April evenings here and was sorry she had not added a topcoat to her mourning wardrobe. She knew she was an oddity in men's trousers and waistcoat, but she rarely wore dresses now. When she did, it felt more like a disguise.

A light caught her attention. *The candle!*

She strode out from under the trees and moved quickly to the back door of the house, where she found the door slightly ajar. *Thank you, Etty.*

She pushed the door open slowly, not wanting to alert anyone with an errant squeak. The door complied in silence, and she walked in, making her way through the darkness by memory, to the parlor at the front of the house.

She paused and listened. All was quiet.

She moved to the casket and slowly lifted the lid, its weight much more than she had expected. *The oak,* she thought. She slid the lid to the side with some effort, and the smell of death rose to greet her. She turned away and took a deep breath before looking in again, but the room was so dimly lit that all she saw was darkness. She tentatively reached a hand in, searching for his waistcoat. Her hand went in farther, and farther, and farther, until it touched wood. *What the —*

"Yes," whispered Etty, coming into the room. "He is gone. A man from Westminster Abbey came just after you left. He and John transferred the body to a grand coffin and loaded it onto a carriage, where it is now, under guard."

"But the notebooks, Etty, the notebooks."

"With him still. The carriage is to take father to Westminster Abbey on the morrow, and then he will be interred there the next day."

Lily sighed. "The 26th? I am lost."

"No, there is still time to retrieve them, Lily."

"What, from Westminster Abbey? How can I possibly do that? It is far too public."

"No, I asked about that. The casket will be kept in storage tomorrow night in the Chapel of St. Faith, a small chapel within the Abbey and not frequented by visitors. That will be your best chance to retrieve the notebooks."

"The night before the ceremony?"

"Yes, exactly."

"But I have never even been in the Abbey. Where is this little chapel, and how do I get in and out without being detected?"

Etty sighed. "I have been there several times. I can show you, but not until tomorrow, when my husband and I are to be in London, along with the rest of the family, of course."

"Husband? You're married?"

Etty chuckled. "More than ten years now, soon to be eleven. You can call me Mrs. Litchfield if you like."

"Oh, my goodness. Children?"

Etty sighed. "No, unfortunately."

Lily thought to say something to console her, but she could tell it would be unwelcome. "Well, then, *Mrs. Litchfield*, shall we say noon?"

"No, we shall say four. I will not be able to break away from Richard until that time. He teaches music at the London Working Men's College, and has a class scheduled."

"Very well, then, four."

Etty nodded. "Now, off with you. I hear Emma stirring."

Lily gave Etty a kiss on the cheek and made her way back through the house, closing the door behind her and then running full out toward her carriage, her breath puffing into the air like a steam engine.

I will have those notebooks!

49

The City Mills, Haggerston, Apartment 132, Monday Evening, October 17.

They had all laughed when DI Harry Morton entered the room, even though he had stolen Bruce's punchline.

"Good to have a laugh at the end of a day like this," Bruce said.

"Indeed," Harry said. "We have ourselves a right monster on our hands, don't we?" *So ends the laughter.*

"So, what do you think, inspector?" Luna asked, Kat nodding vigorously.

Harry looked around for a chair. "Do you mind if I sit?"

"Of course not," Luna said, pointing to the chair opposite the sofa. "Please."

Harry sat down. The red side chair had an IKEA firmness that Harry didn't like. Give him soft and cushy every time. But it did afford a wonderful view of two beautiful women, so he was not about to complain.

Kat was distracting to say the least. She was dressed in tight-fitting black leather shorts and a sheer, see-through black crop top that revealed an underlying black bra that barely covered her nipples. Each shoulder of the crop top included a built-in faux tattoo of a dragon on each shoulder. Red shoes with high spike heels completed her wardrobe. She would have been the first to admit that she referred to them as her "fuck me" shoes. Luna had rolled her eyes at her outfit when she had first walked in, but didn't say anything. It was just Kat being her playful self.

As if that weren't playful enough, she was adorned with a variety of jewelry: several large gold bracelets on each arm, loop earrings in her ears, and a large gold ring that spanned her right hand. Her belly button sparkled from a diamond stud whenever she changed positions. For all this dazzle, the two things that stood out about her were her lips—the top lip a shade of orange, the bottom blood red—and her skin, which was flawless. *Ah, youth*, Harry thought.

Luna, by contrast, was dressed simply: a pair of pale blue slacks made of some kind of shimmering material—he didn't know what—and a long-sleeved white blouse with a high collar. The only jewelry she wore was a silver bracelet, which she jiggled every few seconds, as if she weren't used to wearing it. She would have certainly lost a fashion contest with Kat, but it was Luna, not Kat, that mesmerized him. When he spoke, he spoke to her, so he could drink her in.

"It's a strange story, but it certainly backs up what each of you has told us. Of course, we'll have to validate its authenticity, but I want each of you to know that I believe it to be genuine."

"We thought you would," Luna said. "So now what?"

"As I said earlier, I think the key to this is Jamie Doyle. Mr. Cargo's description of our evidence boxes was spot on, so if this Doyle has it, how did he come by it? Did the monster give it to him? Is *he* the monster? If so, why does he look like any other bloke? Does he transform somehow like a werewolf?"

"Ewww," Kat said. "And don't forget whatever came out of that egg. We're dealing with two monsters, right?"

Harry nodded. "That may well be. I'm hoping the DNA results will give us some answers. If the DNA samples from both sites match, then we're probably dealing with just one monster, which would be plenty as far as I'm concerned. And if the DNA from the sites match the DNA we collected at Jamie's flat and the office, we'll know even more."

"All good questions," said Luna. "And we certainly don't need two monsters. But what if that is exactly what we're dealing with?"

"Normally — and I'm not saying we're dealing with *normal* by any means — normally we would hope to capture one, and then get him to point us to the other." Harry let out a little chuckle. "But how do you capture a monster so powerful, let alone interrogate him — or *it*?"

"Very carefully, I would think," Luna said, and they all laughed.

Harry smiled. "I'm glad you have a sense of humor about this." He looked at each of them in turn. "Now, there's other things that puzzle me."

"Yes?" said Bruce.

"First, why are the documents and shell fragments so important to the monster, important enough for him to kill? What's his motive?"

They all shrugged.

"Second, this process Zhao Yu described of one dragon killing another until it was strong enough to face the Red Dragon. Is that already happening here? I mean, we know that the one son, Zhao Jiao-long, killed the white dragon. Is that why he's here in England now? Is he looking for another dragon to kill?"

"And if that's true," said Luna, "are we dealing with a dragon-man that's potentially going to become more and more powerful?"

"I don't like the sound of that," Kat said. She looked down at the wine glasses. "Inspector, can I offer you some wine?"

Harry started to say something but stopped when he saw Luna and Bruce both giving their heads a little shake and mouthing "no." *I guess I may not be as welcome as I thought.*

"Well," he said, "perhaps another time. On duty, you see. Besides, it's time for me to head back to the office. Might be we have some DNA results." He stood and started for the door.

"Thank you so much, inspector," said Luna. "Would you call us when you know more?"

"Of course, of course. Good evening, then."

They all stood and walked him to the door. When he had left, Kat let out a big sigh. "He's kind of dreamy, don't you think?"

Luna chuckled. "Oh, Kat, you think everyone is dreamy."

"I know," she giggled. "Isn't it wonderful? But I think he's sweeter on you than he is on me. Or did you miss the looks he was giving you?"

"Hey!" said Bruce. "She's taken."

Luna started to join in, but her cell phone began ringing. She dug it out of her slacks and pressed the talk button.

"Hello, Luna Fearnow. Yes? Oh hi, Mr. Pibb, what a surprise."

Kat and Bruce watched the look on her face go from happy to serious.

"Okay, okay, I understand. Go ahead and call the police, and we'll let Inspector Morton know as well."

She hung up. "Bruce, go catch Inspector Morton and bring him back. We've got a problem."

"What kind of problem?" said Bruce.

"A big problem. Now go, quickly!" she shouted.

Bruce ran for the door.

"What is it?" asked Kat.

"Looks like I'll be back in the clown car tomorrow."

50

Boorwick Castle, Ten Miles East of Bedford, Monday Evening, October 17.

Jamie was having a hard time wrapping his head around everything that had been said, but given the current situation, with the whole police force looking for him, he was happy to be in the safety of Bai Li's castle. Still, he had questions.

"Okay," he said, "let's assume I buy everything you've said. What happens next and what exactly will be your role?"

Bai Li smiled, pleased. "For now, you will remain here with us, until such time as the Green Dragon reveals itself. The Inner Council is certain that will be happening very soon, based on the behavior of the Red Dragon, who is like the proverbial canary in the mine on such matters. When the Red Dragon reacts, we will react."

"And what will that mean, exactly?"

The Green Dragon is the dragon of the east. Our guess is that we will find him in England, Scotland, or Scandinavia. But no one is sure. Once he is hatched, his location will be known to us. That is when we will go into action. That is when we will seek him out and kill him."

"And now?"

"For now, we wait. You will stay here with us, learn more about the Green Dragon and its strengths and weaknesses."

"And your role?"

"As I have said, as Sixth Assassin to the Red Dragon, it is my job—and Peng's—to protect you and to kill anyone who gets in our way."

"Yes, you had mentioned that, but who exactly will you be protecting me from?"

Li sat back in his chair. "That is a somewhat longer story, and I will tell it to you in the days ahead. For now, the story in brief. When Emperor Zhu Di died, the pale guardians escaped the city and took up residence in a secret location in the mountains, where they remain today with the Red Dragon. The emperors and governments that followed, including today's ruling government, sought us out and still seek us out. So far, we have kept ahead of them, through stealth and skill."

Peng chimed in. "Tell him how many we have killed."

Li turned on him. "*That* is of no consequence!"

"Wait," said Jamie, "I'd really like to know that."

Li glowered at Peng, then turned back to Jamie. "Just over two hundred, a little less than one a year since we arrived here in 1834."

Jamie's jaw dropped. "No *consequence*, huh? Wow!"

"We are capable of more," said Li. "Peng and I could handle a direct attack by dozens of our enemies. We are assassins, after all."

Jamie nodded. "I get that, but let me ask you something."

"Certainly."

"Why are you called the *sixth* assassin?"

Li bowed his head slightly. "An excellent question. Each of the Pale entrusted with an egg is also an assassin. Your father, for example, was the First Assassin of the Red Dragon. So, four eggs, four assassins."

"Was?" said Jamie.

Well, that was subtle, Li thought. He nodded. "Yes, it is time you knew. Your father is dead, killed by assassins, we think sometime in 1836 or 1837. The last words of an assassin who bragged about it. Bad idea. Last idea."

Jamie shook his head. "I sensed it, but never wanted to accept it. I should have been there."

"No, you could not help but leave." Li could see he was stressed. "Do you need a moment? We can continue our talk later."

Jamie took a deep breath. "No, please continue."

"So, when your father died, you were without a protecting assassin. A new assassin, the fifth, was sent to England the same year you arrived, but as luck would have it, he was killed the moment he stepped off the ship. Carelessness."

Jamie nodded. "And thus you, the sixth assassin."

"Yes, and Peng, the seventh, in the event of my death." He looked over at Peng. "That is, if he should ever complete his training."

Peng did not respond. He just sat there brooding.

Jamie drummed his fingers on the table. "So, let me summarize. I am to kill three more dragons, each protected by an assassin, while being pursued by additional assassins of the Chinese government."

"Yes."

"And all this in order to kill the Red Dragon."

"To become a god."

Jamie laughed sardonically. "Oh, yes, I'd forgotten about the god thing. Well, this looks easy enough."

Bai Li raised a hand. "It does sound daunting."

"Daunting? It sounds absurd!"

"Please calm yourself. Remember, Peng and I have protected you for decades upon decades, through many empires and governments, dispatching more than 200 would-be assassins in the process. You are in good hands, and safe."

Jamie sighed and fell silent, looking down at the table.

"You will be fine, believe me," Li said.

Jamie looked up. "All right, are we done for today? I'm starving."

Bai Li smiled. "Good, I will have Peng prepare us a meal—he is an excellent chef, at least—and we shall call it a day."

"Thank you."

Li turned to Peng. "Your prawns with walnuts would be just the thing."

Peng bowed and left the room.

Li turned back to Jamie. "Now, while he is preparing the food, I wonder if you would show me how you transform from a man to your true self."

Jamie rolled his eyes. "Whatever."

51

Outside Jack's Lorry and Limo, Finsbury Park, Monday Night, October 17.

Darweshi Dewji watched them arrive, the tall blonde in a little Austin Mini, and his target and her boyfriend in an old Land Rover. They had been escorted through the chain-link gate by several agents. MI5, probably, Box 500 men. The local constabulary was there, of course, but it was clear they were not in charge, despite all their flashing lights. No, not in the least. And he thought he detected an agent or two from MI6 as well. The whole plot seemed to be unravelling, and Dewji was not quite sure how to proceed.

He sat there in the car for more than an hour, sorting out what to do next. Clearly, the rigged limousine was off the table. He would have to go after her full on, as quickly and as forcefully as he could. Time was his enemy.

He spotted the three of them coming back through the gate and climbing into the Land Rover. The blonde had apparently decided to leave the Mini behind. Why? And then it came to him. Of course, the chauffer. He wouldn't be able to drive the limousine for several days while they tore it down and reassembled it looking for additional devices. He would be driving the Mini come morning. *Excellent!* Dewji chuckled. *Some limo! This is going to be almost too easy!*

Then Dewji had another thought. He turned to his driver. "Follow that Land Rover, but not too closely. Are the weapons in the trunk?"

The man nodded with a grunt.

"All right, go, go, we don't want to lose them!"

The driver pulled the car out of its parking spot and slowly picked up speed.

Dewji picked up his cell phone and punched in Ahmed's number.

Ahmed's voicemail message began, and Dewji waited patiently for the beep. "My dear Ahmed," he said. "I have your cigars."

52

Thames Foyer, The Savoy, London, Tuesday morning, October 18.

Ahmed sat at his usual table, sipping his second cup of coffee. He had arrived early, hoping that Darweshi Dewji would do the same. Both had what they wanted now, at least Dewji did, and Ahmed was eager to receive his final payment. *Ah, here he comes at last.*

Dewji made his way through the tables, giving Ahmed a big smile as he came up to the table and sat down. "Good morning, my friend."

Ahmed wiped his mouth with a napkin. "I trust all went well?"

Dewji nodded, smiling even more broadly. "Much easier than we had hoped, and all thanks to you."

"So, Luna is—"

"On her way to Tanzania."

Ahmed nodded. "So, our business is complete," he said, "except for one last detail."

"Ah, yes, the details. What would we do without them?"

"Indeed."

Dewji pushed the mobile across the table to Ahmed, who seemed surprised.

"I don't want this back. I thought you would destroy it."

Dewji shrugged. "I thought you might have further use for it. It could not have come cheap."

Ahmed reluctantly took the phone and put it in his suit jacket pocket. "And the money?"

Dewji reached into his suit jacket, then frowned, patting his other pockets. "I seem to have left the envelope in the car. Have another cup of coffee. I will be right back."

Ahmed started to object, but Dewji stood and patted him firmly on the shoulder. "No worries, my friend. I will be but a moment."

Dewji turned and walked slowly back through the chairs, leaving Ahmed sitting there with his mouth open, incredulous.

Ahmed shook his head and looked at his watch. He was overdue at the embassy. His father said he had a matter of "utmost importance" to discuss with him. No doubt it would be a lecture about his gambling debt. When Dewji returned with the cash, that debt would be a thing of history.

He took a sip of coffee. It had a bitter metallic taste, probably from sitting in the silver pot too long. He set his cup down and scanned the dining room for Dewji. *Where the hell was he?*

His shoulder began to ache, a strange sensation of warmth spreading down his arm and up his neck. The light streaming in from the glass cupola seemed to intensify, the people sitting in the tables in front of him blurring into a rainbow of colors, then fading to white.

A diner two tables over took time out from scolding his son about table manners to wonder why the Arab in the expensive suit was staring so intently at him. He would have to have a talk with the maître d'. If they were going to let such people in the dining room, they should at least instruct them on proper manners. He had a mind to punch the man in the face. And by God, he would!

53

The Gladstone, Number 6, Finsbury Park, Tuesday Morning, October 18.

She was kissing him, licking his neck and his chest, and he was not about to stop her. He ran his hand up her bare thigh and pulled her closer, losing himself in the moment.

And then he was awake, Lucifer sitting on his chest, licking him.

"Oh, Lucifer, you've right spoiled a wonderful dream." He wanted to fall back asleep again, but knew he'd never find her again, not even in his dream life. He pulled Lucifer off his chest and set him down next to him on the sofa. He had been so tired when he returned from Jack's that he had turned on the telly and fallen asleep in the middle of a vampire movie.

Another movie was playing now. Some kind of werewolf movie, the man changing to a wolf with probably the worst special effects that Pibb had ever seen. He grabbed the flipper and turned it off.

He checked his watch. Just enough time to shower, dress, have a quick bite, and be on his way to pick up Luna and Kat. It was going to be odd trying to be a chauffeur in a tiny old Austin Mini, but fun as well. Of all the cars he had ever owned or driven, the Austin Mini was his clear favorite.

Lucifer let out a mournful meow. "All right, all right, I know my priorities."

He went to the kitchen, grabbed a tin off the shelf, opened it, and dropped the gelatinous mass of tuna parts into a clean bowl, Lucifer rubbing against his leg all the while. *It's good to be appreciated.* And then he thought of the woman in his dream, and sighed.

"Luci, have I ever told you about Montore's Maxim?" Lucifer looked up briefly and then resumed eating.

"It says that love expands to fill the available hearts. How's that for bollocks?"

Lucifer gave the bowl one last lick and scurried away.

"I could use some of that expansion right about now."

He picked up the bowl and put it in the sink. "Ah, the bachelor's life."

His mobile rang. "Pibb here." It was Luna. "Yes, madam, no problem. See you at 10:00, then."

He put the mobile back on the counter where he had dumped his pockets the night before.

The night before. The whole evening seemed to be occupied by questioning and more questioning, when it was he and Luna and Kat and Bruce who had had the questions. Who put a kill switch and maybe a bomb in the car? Why? Who was it intended for? What now?

The spooks from MI5 and MI6 were in a feeding frenzy on turf issues, so they had all been questioned three times, including an interview with the local constabulary. The long and short of it was the authorities had to impound the limo and give it a more thorough search before it could be returned to Luna. Luna had objected, of course, but there was no help for it.

Fortunately, Luna had already anticipated that, having Kat come along to drop off the Mini for him to drive. After the questioning, they had jumped into Bruce's old Range Rover and headed home, leaving Pibb with the Mini. He decided to leave it at Jack's for the night rather than try to find street parking so late in the evening.

He looked at his watch. Time for that shower.

54

Boorwick Castle, Ten Miles East of Bedford, Tuesday Morning, October 18.

Jamie stared across the table at Li and Peng as they ate their breakfast. Li's reaction to his transformation the evening before, the demonstration he had requested, had been dramatic. His arrogance had dropped away, and Jamie could tell that it had been replaced by reasoned respect and barely controlled fear. Li could no longer hold Jamie's stare, quickly looking away.

Jamie thought, *Perhaps I can be a god*. He cleared his throat to get their attention. They both looked up and set down their chopsticks. If anything, Peng seemed more nervous than Li.

"Am I to assume that I must stay here, for however long—weeks, months, years, decades, *centuries*—until the Green Dragon emerges from its shell?"

Li nodded, then shook his head. "It will *not* be centuries or decades or years. If the Inner Council is correct, it could be no more than a few days, perhaps a week."

"What of my things?"

"They are lost to you. You do not dare return."

"What shall I wear?"

"Peng is an excellent tailor. He has made clothing for you."

Jamie pounded the table. "I don't see why I should be restricted in any way! You've seen what I can become. Why would I fear a few policemen?"

"Because there are *more* than policemen out there."

"The assassins?"

"Yes, and the military. You do not dare reveal your location. We must bide our time and then move quickly but stealthily to the location of the Green Dragon."

Jamie shook his head in frustration. "All right, I see your point. But if I want to go out, I will go out!"

Li started to object, but Jamie waved him off. "Tell me about the Green Dragon. What exactly will I be facing?"

Li appreciated the change of subject. He wiped his mouth with a napkin and pushed his plate aside. "Peng, fetch the manual."

"Manual?" said Jamie.

"That is what we call it. It describes in great detail the strengths and weaknesses of each dragon you must face: green, yellow, and blue. And then red, of course. It will be a good way to pass the time."

"All right."

Peng pushed back from the table and left the room.

"Good," Li said. "While you read, we will monitor the current situation and see if there is any news from the Inner Council."

Jamie shook his head. "I'll read the manual later. Right now, I have an errand to run."

"Errand?"

"A score to settle. It will only take an hour or so."

Li stood up, fists clenched at his sides. "You cannot leave!"

Jamie laughed. "And who will stop me?"

55

The Chapel of St. Faith, Westminster Abbey, London, 10:55 p.m., Tuesday, April 25, 1882.

The chapel was exactly as Etty had described it, though its beauty was somewhat muted by the dim light provided by two old-fashioned lanterns set on the floor near Darwin's coffin. It was a small apartment, long and narrow, and mostly bare, with a groined and vaulted roof. Darwin's coffin sat in the center, covered with a black drape.

Lily, dressed in peasant clothing and carrying a large spray of white flowers, had passed by the one guard easily, saying only "flowers for Mr. Darwin." The guard had waved her through and then turned away, leaving her alone with the coffin. She had been quick at her work, throwing back the black drape, opening the coffin, and extracting the notebooks.

She put a hand on Darwin's chest. "Farewell, dear friend, and thank you for these. I promise to keep them safe and away from the eyes of man."

Minutes later, she was safely back in her carriage, speeding away from London and into the countryside. As her driver urged the horses on, Lily tried her best to begin reading the notebooks, but the light was too dim and the road too rough to accommodate reading. The best she could do was count the notebooks, which strangely numbered seven.

She would sort it all out when she got to the inn.

56

Outside Jack's Lorry and Limo, Finsbury Park, Tuesday Morning, October 18.

The walk from his flat to Jack's seemed easier this morning, perhaps because he had had the first decent breakfast in weeks. He felt full and energized.

The Austin Mini was where they had left it, but the bonnet was up. He could see Jack leaning in, looking at the engine.

"What's up, Jack?" he said walking up to the car.

"Morning, Ponty," he said with a quick smile. "I thought you said this was a restoration."

"Right. Isn't it?"

Jack chuckled. "Not at all. Have a look."

Pibb looked at the engine and whistled. "Oh, my, what have we here?"

"Ha! Where do I begin? Someone's stuffed the biggest engine they could find in here. BMW. Turbocharged. Fuel injected. Tuned exhaust. Six-speed trannie. All-wheel drive. Nothing Austin about it. Plus you have a racing suspension, heavy duty shocks, and look at this—those new run-flat tires. This is a right screamer."

Pibb smiled and rubbed his hands together. "And I get to drive her." He reached up and closed the bonnet. "I must be off, Jack."

"Enjoy your day, mate." He turned and walked away.

Pibb climbed into the car. He could tell from the sound it made when he started it that today was going to be a good day. He eased the car into the street, popped the clutch, and sped away.

Dewji watched the Mini pull out and accelerate. "Let's go!" he yelled into his mobile. The three black BMWs pulled out of their parking spaces and sped away.

57

Briefing Room 3, Scotland Yard, Tuesday Morning, October 18.

Detective Chief Inspector Falvey was running late, but had instructed Harry to begin the briefing without him. He cleared his throat and raised a hand to silence the room. "Let's begin, shall we?"

The room continued to buzz. News of the rigged limo had already raced through the ranks.

"Gentlemen," he shouted. "Let. Us. Begin."

The buzzing stopped.

"To save time, let me summarize the forensics on the current case, and then I'll bring you up to speed on what transpired last evening in regards to Ms. Fearnow's limousine."

He paused. Everyone was nodding.

"Right. As to the hairs found at the scenes. Some were from Ms. Fearnow, as expected, and some are presumed to be from the killer. In addition, the hairs at the crime scenes matched the hairs found at Jamie Doyle's office and flat. Most important, the hairs are not human, and like the egg fragments, can be traced to no known species."

He looked over at Hermione Divers, who was nodding and smiling.

"No big surprise, given what we've seen on the enhanced videos and from social media. We're dealing with a monster, part man and part, well, part dragon."

He scanned the room. "Questions?"

He knew there would be none. The questions would come later, of course, but right now the assembled teams were more interested in the limousine and what that might mean.

"Okay, as I'm sure many of you already know, we had an incident last night with Ms. Fearnow's limousine, a vehicle that she had recently purchased — at a very low price, I might add — from an Ahmed Abhoud, who just happens to be the son of the Saudi ambassador. Needless to say, MI5, MI6, and all people diplomatic were called in, and there are still some jurisdictional issues, as you might well imagine."

Several officers laughed.

"It was rigged with a kill switch and two mobile-triggered gas canisters that would have left the occupants unconscious long enough for a kidnapping, or worse, to take place. Our initial thought was that the device was intended for someone at the Saudi embassy, either Ahmed Abhoud or perhaps the ambassador himself."

He paused and scanned the room. "But we've had a recent development that may indicate that Ahmed Abhoud was actually behind, or party to, whatever plot was at work. He was found dead this morning at the Savoy, at his breakfast table, the triggering mobile in his pocket."

Several officers raised their hands. "Hold your questions until I finish."

The hands went down.

"Initially, there was some confusion about manner of death. People in the dining room said another diner had punched Abhoud in the face and that Abhoud had fallen lifeless to the floor. Turns out, though, that he was already dead. Preliminary thinking is poison of some kind."

More hands were raised. "Patience. One more item of business before I can address your questions. We've been fortunate to obtain security camera footage of Abhoud's last moments. Seems he had a visitor at breakfast, who may be able to shed some light on the situation. Harkins, would you kill the lights?"

Detective Harkins stood up, went to the wall, and turned off the lights. The video began.

"Here we see the man approach the table and sit down. Something, we think the mobile, is passed from him to Abhoud, who looks like he doesn't want to accept it. Then the man pats his pockets and leaves the table, giving Abhoud a friendly pat on the back. The man never returns. Now, firstly — "

Sergeant Kadika leaped to his feet. "I know that man!"

"Sergeant?" said Harry.

"That man, sir, he is from my home country, Tanzania, and he is known as *the harvester*."

"Harvester?"

"Yes, sir, he harvests the blood and organs of albinos. Sir, they are targeting Ms. Fearnow!"

A chill went up Harry's spine.

"Bennie, you're with me. Tompkins, alert Falvey, and send as many available officers to Fearnow's home and office. Firearms authorized! Hurry!"

Harry grabbed Bennie by the arm and pulled him toward the door. "Move!"

He grabbed his mobile and pulled up "Fearnow" in his contact list. Her phone number popped up and he pressed call. The phone rang four times and then her message came on.

Shite, he thought, *shite, shite, shite!*

58

Outside The City Mills, Haggerston, Tuesday Morning, October 18.

Pibb could not believe his good fortune. Driving the Mini had been a dream and had brought back memories of his youth, when he drove rally cars on the international circuit. Why had he given up cars for boxing? It baffled him now.

The only thing that could have possibly broken his reverie would have been a rainy day, but the weather was cooperating. A relatively cloud-free day, with mild temperatures.

He had somehow managed to drive to Haggerston well above the speed limit without encountering a single police car. It had been pure exhilaration: the roar of the engine, the silky smooth transmission, the way the car cornered, flat and tight. If he had had this car when he was young, he would have been unbeatable. *Or mayhaps, dead*, he thought.

Throughout the drive, he had noticed a black BMW trying to keep up, and it couldn't, which delighted him no end. *You'll need more than a stock BMW to keep up with me today, you git!*

He downshifted, braked, and drove past the throng of reporters and cameras that continued to camp out in front of Luna's building. Their numbers had grown considerably, and they seemed restive. He saw several popular commentators standing in front of cameras and bright lights, their faces orange with makeup. *Bollocks!*

He drove to the designated pickup spot, Luna and Kat immediately opening a side door to the building and racing for the car, Kat carrying what looked like two long sticks and a little bundle of twigs. *Crikey, she's beautiful. Runs like a gazelle!*

They were both wearing black yoga pants and brightly colored running shoes. Kat's top was some sort of body-hugging black athletic jacket with fluorescent green stripes down the sleeves, and she had pulled her hair back into a pony tail that bounced charmingly as she ran. Luna tried to keep up, one hand on her fedora as her knee-length red jacket flapped in the wind.

Kat jumped in the back seat with the sticks—*are those arrows?*—and Luna scrambled into the front seat next to Pibb.

"Welcome, ladies. Click those seatbelts, we're off!"

He threw the gear shift into first and sped away, working his way through the gear progressions until Luna's building had disappeared.

"Whoa, Mr. Pibb, not so fast!" Luna shouted.

He eased back on the accelerator. "Yes, madam, sorry madam, it's just this car, it's a blooming masterpiece."

Kat laughed. "What did I tell you? It is so awesome!"

"Well, there's no rush now," said Luna, "we're media free."

Her cell phone began ringing. She ignored it. "Sorry, media, no calls today, thank you very much."

Pibb chuckled. "Well done, madam. Now, where shall we go this fine morning?"

Luna dug into her purse and pulled out her address book. "First stop will be a photo studio on Flemington Street. Let's see, yes, number 32. That's where you'll drop me. Then you and Kat will be going to the archery range."

Archery? Pibb shook his head, downshifted, braked, and did a quick U-turn. "Then we'll need to reverse our steps a bit."

As he began to accelerate, three black BMWs shot by them, going in their previous direction. *That's odd.*

He looked in the rearview mirror. They were braking hard and turning around. *This doesn't look right.*

"Hold on, ladies, we seem to have a tail."

Luna and Kat looked over their shoulders at the pursuing cars.

"Reporters, do you think?" said Kat.

"Must be," said Luna. "Mr. Pibb, do you think you could lose them?"

"With pleasure, madam."

"But not in a Princess Diana sort of way," said Kat.

"No, miss."

He changed gears and floored it, the little car going nearly airborne as they crested a small hill. The pursuing cars seemed to drop back. When they were out of sight, he would make a sharp right and try to lose them.

59

Inside a Police Car, Racing through London, Tuesday Morning, October 18.

Harry slammed the mobile on his leg and punched the roof of the car.

"*Bollocks!* No one is answering!" He had tried them all several times, but without success.

Sergeant Kadika tried to calm him. "We will be there momentarily, sir. If your hunch is right, in plenty of time."

Harry shook his head. "I'm not good on hunches, Bennie. That's my history, anyway."

"It will be fine, sir." He patted the H&K MP55F 9mm submachine gun lying on the seat next to him.

The car crested a hill and went airborne. "I see you took the driving course."

"Yes, sir."

Harry looked over at Bennie. He had not said more than a few words to this gentle giant in the past year, and yet here they were on perhaps the most important action he had ever taken, not knowing much about the man next to him. Could he count on him?

"How do you know this harvester person?"

Bennie sighed. "His name is Darweshi Dewji. I encountered him several years ago, when I was a teenager living in Tanzania and dreaming of England."

"Encountered? How?"

"I was asleep at home and heard screams and scuffling coming from our kitchen. Three men, including Dewji, were standing in the kitchen with machetes. My parents were tied up. My sister, Zahra, was on the floor, covered in blood. They had chopped off one of her hands and were pouring gasoline on her bleeding stump. Dewji saw me, offered me the can of gasoline, and said, 'Here, burn it. It will stop the bleeding.'"

Harry was wide-eyed, near speechless. "And? And?—"

"And then they were gone. I still remember her screams when I did it, and the smell."

"Did she live?"

Bennie nodded, a tear rolling down his cheek. "That time, yes. But they came back, and then Zahra was gone. Forever."

"Your sister was an albino."

"Yes."

"In the Fearnow interview. She attacked you, and you said nothing."

"No, sir. She needed to vent. My sister did so many times. They do not have easy lives. It would not have been right."

Harry could feel his heart beating in his chest. "Well, let's get that bastard."

Bennie smiled gamely. "Yes, sir, let's do that."

Harry slid the magazine into his Glock 17 and pulled back the slide as Bennie downshifted the car and made a quick right turn. The address was dead ahead.

60

Austin Mini, Streets of London, Tuesday Morning, October 18.

Pibb was trying his best to shake them, but the BMWs were still on his tail.

"Hold onto something, ladies, I'm going to try a spin move."

"Mr. Pibb, I don't think—"

He ignored Luna, whipping the wheel to the left sharply and pulling on the emergency brake. The car whipped around, and he managed to accelerate down the street in the opposite direction before the BMWs had a chance to respond.

Kat turned to look at the BMWs disappearing behind them. "Ha! Well done, Mr. Pibb!"

Pibb smiled, checked the mirror—no BMWs in sight—and made a sharp left turn. "Are you all right, madam?" he said to Luna.

Luna shook her head. "Now, yes, but I almost peed my pants back there."

They all laughed.

"Mr. Pibb, it seems we've lost them," said Luna. "Let's head to the studio so you can drop me off."

"And then, Mr. Pibb," said Kat, "I have a special treat for you. Ever shot a bow and arrow?"

"No, miss."

"Well, I have two bows back here and a dozen new hunting arrows, sharp as all razor hell, and we're going to give them a chance to prove themselves."

"Yes, miss, that would be fun." *What the bloody hell?*

He made a right, then a left, and drove down Flemington Street, coming to a stop in front of the studio. "Here we are."

The BMWs seemed to come from out of nowhere, one pulling up to block the front of the car, another to block the rear, and the third to block the side. They were trapped.

Two black men got out of each car and aimed pistols and shotguns at the Mini. A seventh man carrying a machete emerged from the back of the BMW blocking the side of the Mini, and smiled. He was obviously the leader.

"Do not shoot. I want them alive," he said to the men.

He looked over at Luna, Kat, and Pibb. "Please step out of the car and raise your hands."

Luna turned to Pibb and Kat. "Stay where you are. It's me they want."

"But madam—" Pibb said.

"Just do it, Mr. Pibb. I know what I'm doing."

She stepped out of the car and took a few steps toward the leader, who was not amused.

"I said for all of you to get out of the car—*now!*"

Luna took another step toward him. If she could just get close enough, she could take him out.

One of his men stepped in front of her, blocking her. She could smell his cologne, which smelled of rubbing alcohol. An aftershave, then.

"It's me you want," she said. "Leave them out of this."

"Ms. Indigo, it *is* you I want, yes, but the others—the others are a complication, and I hate complications."

He nodded to the man closest to the car, who shot one round into the sky. "Get out, now!" he shouted.

Pibb and Kat opened their doors, each stepping out, leaving the doors open. As she got out, Kat slid the bow and arrows within reach. If they were going to kill her, she would at least have a chance to do some damage.

61

Parking Lot, British Geological Survey, Nottingham, Tuesday Morning, October 18.

Bruce sat in the Range Rover, collecting his thoughts for the meeting he knew Old Nozzle would want first thing. He had arrived early enough to check in at his flat, take a shower, and put on a suit. He would be firm with Old Nozzle this time, and the suit would help him act the part.

He and Luna had not had time for that talk about his first meeting with Dr. Shepherd. He still winced at the words she had spoken to him, but if all went well at work today, if he held his ground, their call this evening would go well.

He glanced at his watch. Still a little early. And then he saw Old Nozzle walking across the parking lot toward him, a big smile on his face. He waved at Bruce, beckoning him.

Bruce climbed out of the car, locked it, and started walking toward his superior, straightening his tie as he walked. When they closed to twenty meters apart, he decided to take the initiative.

"Good morning, sir!" he said as heartily as he could.

Old Nozzle smiled and started to say something, but in the next instant, his head left his body, blood spurting everywhere as he dropped like a sack of stones.

Bruce looked up to see the dragon-man wheeling in the sky, ready to make another pass. He turned and ran for the entrance to the building, thirty meters away. He could just make it, but he had to give it his all.

The security guard saw him running toward the door, and what was swooping down on him from behind. He raced to open the door, but as soon as he touched it, the door was awash in blood.

He heard a shriek and then there was silence.

62

Flemington Street, London, Tuesday Morning, October 18.

Bennie turned the corner and accelerated down Flemington. He could immediately see what they had most feared: Luna, Kat, and Pibb surrounded by armed men.

"Sir?"

"Yes, I see it. Take out the man in the street and ram the car to the left of the Mini."

"Backup, sir? They should be here soon."

"No time. We have to go now."

"Yes, sir." Bennie stepped on the gas and accelerated toward the cars.

The man in the street saw the car at the last second, turned, and fired three quick shots, shattering the windscreen and spraying glass on Harry and Bennie. An instant later his body was flying through the air and the police car was ramming the rear of the BMW, pushing it forward.

Then everything seemed to slow down. Harry and Bennie jumped out of the car, firing as they ran. One of the men dropped immediately, firing his shotgun in the air as he fell. And then Harry saw the most amazing thing: Luna disarming another man, taking him down in a lightning quick move, and snapping his neck. Then Pibb took down another assailant, taking him out with a fierce fusillade of punches.

Harry was about to fire at the three remaining men, but two of them dropped immediately, arrows sprouting from their chests.

The remaining man, the one with the machete, began running for one of the BMWs.

"It's Dewji!" Harry raised his gun and took aim. "Stop! Now!"

Dewji continued to run. He was almost at the car. Out of the corner of his eye, Harry could see Kat racing across the roof of the Mini, drawing back her bow. *Jesus!*

Bennie pulled down Harry's arm. "I've got this!"

He ran after him, gaining ground quickly. Just as Dewji reached the car, he turned on Bennie and began to swing the machete. An arrow hit his wrist, and he dropped the machete clanging to the ground.

Bennie stooped to pick it up, and Harry yelled at him.

"Stay down, he's got a gun!" He could tell from the profile of the gun, even at this distance, that the man's gun was a 50-caliber semiauto, more gun than their protective vests could handle. Harry took aim, but it was too late. Bennie had stood back up and was now blocking Harry's shot.

Dewji began firing, hitting Bennie twice in the chest, staggering him, but he wouldn't go down. A second arrow hit Dewji in the shoulder and he dropped the gun. Bennie saw his chance, moved forward, and swung the machete again and again.

"For Zahra, for Zahra, for Zahra!" he screamed.

Dewji's head dropped to his chest, near severed, held on by nothing more than a tendon; then his whole body dropped to the ground, fountains of blood pulsing from his neck. Bennie dropped the machete, took a step toward Harry, gave him a faint smile, and collapsed on the road.

Harry and Kat raced up to help him, but it was too late. He wasn't breathing and Harry couldn't get a pulse. Bennie's eyes stared blankly at the sky.

"Bloody hell!" screamed Harry. He reached over and closed Bennie's eyes.

"Goddammit!" cried Kat, dropping to her knees next to Bennie's body.

Harry looked back at the scene. Six dead, one unconscious, and two more brave people walking toward him.

63

Royal London Hospital, London, Tuesday Afternoon, October 18.

Luna, Kat, and Pibb sat quietly in the waiting room, hoping for word of Bruce's condition. Doctors had stabilized him at Queen's Medical Centre in Nottingham, and then he had been taken by air ambulance to the Royal London, where a team of surgeons had been assembled at short notice. He was in surgery now, had been for some hours, and if the look on the face of the nurse who had greeted them was any measure, in grave condition.

Luna was numb with fear, and she was angry with herself, and felt guilty, that she'd been so harsh with Bruce about his talk with Old Nozzle. If only they had talked that through last night.

She was also having a hard time coming to grips with the story DI Morton had told her about Detective Sergeant Kadika. *Why did I say those terrible things to him?*

Pibb dropped the old automotive magazine he'd been trying to read onto the little magazine table in front of them. He pointed down the hall, where two doors had swung open.

"Here he comes."

They all looked up and watched the surgeon walking toward them, pulling off his operating mask, and frowning. They started to stand, but he motioned them to remain seated.

"Are you the wife?" he asked Kat.

Luna stood up. "No, it's me, his girlfriend. We're not married yet."

The surgeon frowned. "I'm Doctor Smythe."

Luna nodded. "Yes?"

He sighed. "The good news is that he's alive."

Luna put a hand to her trembling lips and fought off tears.

"The bad news is that he's dropped into a coma."

"What?"

"It sometimes happens with severe injuries like this."

"Will he, will he . . ."

"Survive? Yes, I think so, but it could go either way, I'm afraid. The next few days will tell the tale. He's stable now, so that's good."

"How bad is it?"

The doctor took a deep breath and glanced at each of them.

"He suffered two fractured legs, six broken ribs, two cracked vertebrae, a collapsed lung, extensive lacerations on his back and head, and severe head trauma, which is the injury we'll have to watch most closely."

Luna put her face in her hands and choked back tears.

The doctor put a hand on her shoulder. "If you need a few minutes—"

She reached out and took the surgeon's hands in hers. "No. No, I'll be all right. I just want to thank you for what you've done—keeping him alive."

He shook his head. "It's too early for thanks. Besides, the person you should really thank is that security guard. If not for him, Mr. Cargo would have bled out on the scene."

"Can I at least see him?"

"Not yet, I'm afraid. Tomorrow perhaps."

He looked at the three of them. "Do you live nearby?"

They nodded. "Pretty close," said Luna.

"There's nothing more you can do here today. Go home, get some rest. We will call you if there's any change in his condition overnight."

Luna looked from Kat to Pibb, and they both nodded. "All right."

Her stomach twisted into a tight knot.

64

The Banks of Loch Ness, Just Outside Drumnadrochit, Scotland, Tuesday Afternoon, October 18.

Ian MacKay, age 12, and his younger brother Angus, age 6, trudged along the edge of the loch, picking up flat stones and skipping them across the water, something they did day in and day out after school.

A cold breeze was blowing across the loch, creating little ripples in its dark, mirrored surface, which seemed to shatter brightly with every skip of a stone. In the distance, they could see the trees in all their fall splendor — yellows and oranges and browns.

Ian was big for his age, and stout, with the red hair and green eyes of his father. His little brother, who was known affectionately as "Shrimp" by his father, was tiny by comparison, but with the same color hair and eyes as his brother. Small as he was, though, he was a feisty little bugger.

"That was four, Bean!" Ian shouted after the rock had stopped skipping. His brother's name may have been Angus, but he called him by his middle name, Bean, anyway. Bean just seemed too small and frail to carry around a name like Angus.

Bean was having none of it. "I count three."

"Four!"

"*Three!*" He may have been smaller than his big brother, but he could bloody shout louder than him.

Ian shook his head and trudged on, working his way up the amber hill away from the loch. When he crested the hill, he stopped.

"Bean, come and see!"

Bean dropped his handful of stones and raced up the hillside. They both looked down at the scene below. A car had apparently missed a turn in the road and crashed.

The boys looked at one another and raced for the wreck, Ian arriving first and quickly circling the car. Even from a distance, Bean could see the man inside the car was dead. The car had apparently flipped several times, crushing the man. There was blood everywhere.

"Stay back, Bean!" Ian shouted, and then bent over and threw up.

Bean stopped in his tracks. "Is he dead?"

Ian nodded and wiped his mouth on his shirt. "We better get home and tell someone."

"Aye, that would seem wise," said Bean, echoing a phrase his mother used whenever Bean happened upon a good solution. "Do you suppose he's been here long?"

Ian approached the car and put his hand tentatively on the engine. "Aye, engine's cold." He sniffed the air. "And thing's don't smell very good."

"A long while, then?"

"Maybe. Dunno. The drop off would have blocked anyone's view from the road, though."

A soft purring sound came from the back seat of the car. "Here, what's this?" said Ian. He peered into the car, and then jumped back.

"Holy shite!" he squealed. "Come look!"

Bean walked up to the backseat window of the car and got up on tiptoe to look in. He gasped.

He dropped back down. "Is it?" he said.

Ian giggled. "Aye, I think so."

Bean got up on tiptoe again and had a second look. "It's a little Nessie!"

65

The City Mills, Haggerston, Apartment 132, Friday Evening, October 21.

Three days had passed since the shootout and the attack on Bruce. Luna had spent most of her time at the hospital on Wednesday, but when Bruce's parents had arrived from Michigan on Thursday morning, she had spent less and less time there.

In truth, they didn't like her and had immediately blamed her for all that had happened. She had lured him to London, they had said, and now look what had happened. Of course, all this was code for, *"We don't want our son to marry a fucking albino!"*

When they had said that, she had stood up and told them to go fuck themselves, and she didn't regret it now in the least. What she regretted was that all the medical decisions were now in their hands, and she had no doubt they would pull the plug on Bruce with the merest suggestion from the medical team.

Now, on Friday evening, after a long photo shoot — she just wasn't into it — she had invited Pibb and Kat up for a drink, and they had quickly accepted, knowing she did not want to be alone.

All three sat slumped on the sofa, sipping at Duct Tape Chardonnay and watching a news channel set on mute. Three days later the shootout was still big news. The loop showing DI Morton at the scene, discussing what had happened, had come and gone several times, as had brief images of the three of them sitting in the back of a police van, wrapped in blankets, looking like refugees fresh over the border.

Pibb took a sip of the wine and screwed up his mouth. "Has a bit of a *twang* to it, doesn't it?"

"What?" Kat said.

"The wine. Seems a bit off."

Kat took a sip. "It's fine."

"Really? Not much of a wine man myself. Don't suppose you have any beer, madam?"

Luna nodded. "In the fridge. Bruce loves beer."

Pibb stood up and walked into the kitchen.

She took a deep breath and tried to calm herself. "What a cluster fuck this week has been."

Kat nodded. "You got that right."

Pibb came back and sat down. He hated to see them so glum, so he decided to do his best to cheer them up, if only a little. "This may not be the best time to say this, but I have to say I was amazed by both of you when everything went bollocks."

He looked at Luna. "The way you disarmed and took down that bloke. I've never seen anyone move so quickly. It was brilliant!"

Luna managed a weak smile. "Training."

"And you, miss," he said, turning to Kat, "You are a right Robin Hood, you are. You will definitely have to show me how to do that!"

Kat shook her head. "If only. I just wish I had those last two shots back. I was aiming at his chest both times, and my arrows went astray. Detective Sergeant Kadika would be alive now if it weren't for that."

"No," said Pibb. "Don't beat yourself up. No one could have done more. And I truly *want* you to teach me how to do that running, shooting thing you do. Amazing."

Kat gave him a sweet smile. "Okay, we'll do that."

Luna suddenly jumped up and pointed at the television. "Wait, what's that? Turn on the sound!"

Pibb grabbed the flipper and took the television off mute as Luna moved closer to the TV so she could see more clearly. Two young boys were being interviewed by an attractive female reporter. One of them was holding something; a small green animal, some sort of lizard, was wriggling in his arms.

"And here's the proof right here, John. If this isn't a baby Nessie, I don't know what it could be."

The camera zoomed in on the animal. Kat, Luna, and Pibb all leaned closer to the TV in unison, Luna's nose almost touching it. "Do you think?" said Luna.

Pibb nodded. "Absolutely."

"No question," said Kat.

The reporter signed off and the face of an overly jolly anchorman came on. "Wow, with all this talk of dragons and dragon-men lately, it is just amazing that amidst all this death and mayhem we come upon a story that could finally solve the mystery of Loch Ness."

He turned to another camera and gave it his best anchorman smile. "I'm John Dawson, and that *was* the news. Good night!"

Luna turned off the television.

"Are you thinking what I'm thinking?" she said, pacing back and forth in front of them, suddenly animated.

"The Green Dragon?" said Kat.

"Yes! Which means?" said Luna.

"Which means," said Pibb, "the dragon-man, Jamie Doyle if you will, will be heading for Scotland."

"So that's where I'll be heading, too," said Luna.

Kat was taken aback. "But what about Bruce?"

Luna shook her head. "We can't do anything for him here, and I can't stand to be around his parents. What I want is to kill the bastard that put him in the hospital — *Jamie*."

"But what if the hospital calls?" said Kat.

"We'll stop there first thing tomorrow and get an update on his condition. And if we decide to go at that point, we can always double back and deal with any change in his condition, good or bad. Right now, though, I don't think we can just sit around here while that beast is on the move. This may be our only chance."

"I'm with you," said Pibb, "but wouldn't it be best to let the authorities handle this?"

Luna sighed. "Well, I'm not going to stop them from doing their job, but I don't want to risk losing this opportunity while they haggle about who's in charge. Besides, I know Jamie well — he likes me, *a lot* — and that might be just the edge we'll need to take him down."

"That makes sense," Pibb said, nodding. "Let's do it."

"That's a long trip in the Mini," said Kat. "Not much in the way of storage."

"Not a problem," said Pibb. "Jack says they've returned the limo. He's giving it a good wash-up, so I can pick you both up first thing in the morning."

"I say we take both cars," said Luna.

"Yes, both have their charms," said Pibb.

Kat shrugged. "Works for me."

Luna turned to Kat. "Is that Scotland shoot still a go?"

Kat beamed. "Oh, yeah, starts Monday."

"Good, we can use that as cover. Okay, Kat, take Mr. Pibb home. Then get packing, including all the bows and arrows you have."

"Right," Kat said, standing to leave.

"I have some Shaolin weapons that may come in handy, too," said Luna. "Mr. Pibb, be here early, say 7:00. We have a long drive."

Pibb chuckled, then got a worried look on his face.

"What?" said Luna.

"Do you mind if I bring along Lucifer?"

66

Royal London Hospital, London, Saturday Morning, October 22.

Luna checked in at the nurse's station and asked about Bruce's condition. The chief nurse, a stout woman in her fifties with the bearing of a drill sergeant, checked the charts, then paged the doctor on call.

"He should be right along," she said, checking her watch. "About finished with his early morning rounds, I should think."

She pointed at a chair against the wall. "Have a seat, if you like."

Luna paced for a couple of minutes, but then walked over to the seat and sat down. That, apparently, was all that was needed to make the doctor suddenly appear. What her cousin called, somewhat crassly, her "butt button," that special device that makes people appear as soon as you sit down. Luna made a mental note to apprise Mr. Pibb of this new law, the Butt Button Law.

The doctor was young, too young it seemed to Luna, to be handling Bruce's case. Where in hell had Dr. Smythe disappeared to? In the past three days, she had not seen him once.

"Good morning," the doctor said. "How can I be of help?"

Luna stood. "I'm checking on the condition of Bruce Cargo."

"Yes?"

"It's just that I may have to go out of town for a while," she said, "but I won't if there's been a change in his condition."

The doctor glanced down at a chart. "Nothing has changed. How long had you planned to be away?"

Luna sighed. "I don't know for sure. Could be a week or so, maybe longer."

"I think you'd be safe to go. I wouldn't expect him to come out of this coma any time soon."

"What does Dr. Smythe say?"

"The surgeon?"

"Yes, has he even *seen* Bruce since the operation?"

The doctor looked at the chart and nodded. "Yes, several times, mostly late in the day after he's completed his surgery schedule."

"Any comments from him in that chart of yours? Any new instructions? Concerns? Anything?"

The doctor dropped the chart to his side. "He made a few changes in the level of certain medications, but his last instruction was for us to — in his words — *maintain and monitor*."

"I see," she said, nodding. "Sounds like it would be safe for me to go, then?"

"I would think so. Do we have your mobile number?"

"Yes, of course."

"Well, then, we can certainly give you a call if there's any change. And, please, call us at any time."

Luna thanked the doctor and walked down the hall to Bruce's room. A nurse was hanging a fresh bag of medications.

"Good morning, madam," she said.

"Morning," Luna said.

The nurse gave her a quick smile, nodded, and walked out of the room, leaving her alone with Bruce.

Oh, Bruce. She could see his face, which was at peace, but everything else looked like something out of a horror film. Monitors, tubes, pulleys, ropes, all manner of devices to support his broken bones and keep him fixed in place.

She moved to the side of the bed and took his hand in hers.

"Oh, Bruce, I'm so glad you can't see all this."

She had a sudden thought and laughed despite herself.

"Yes, I think you'd say the *situation is grim.*"

Her lips began to quiver and a tear ran down her cheek. She leaned in and kissed him softly on his cheek, the tear dropping to his cheek and falling away into the crisp folds of the sheets. All the lines on the monitors continued their steady march across the screens.

She took a deep breath.

"Okay, then, there's something I have to tell you. You won't like it, but there's no help for it—I'm determined, and you know how damned stubborn I can be."

A monitor beeped twice, then stopped, distracting her briefly. *What do all these things mean?*

"Kat and I and Mr. Pibb are going on a little *adventure* in Scotland. We're going to find Jamie and make him pay for—for *this.*"

Bruce's eyelids seemed to quiver. Did she imagine that?

"Yes, of course, I'll be careful."

She squeezed his hand. "Now, your job is to get well. Don't worry, the doctors will call me as soon as you wake up, and I'll be here in a flash."

She patted his hand. "One other thing, mister. I know this may be a break with tradition, but to hell with that. It's about time one of us said it, don't you think?"

She lifted his hand and kissed it. "Will you marry me, Bruce Cargo?"

A monitor beeped.

"I'll take that as a yes," she said and carefully laid his hand back on the bed, stroking it one last time.

Moments later she was walking out of the hospital, brushing away the last of her tears. She could see Mr. Pibb smiling at her and opening the back door to the limo.

"How is he, madam?"

"The same." She ducked her head and got into the limo, Lucifer jumping on her lap immediately.

Mr. Pibb closed the door and gave Kat, who was in the Mini behind them, a thumbs up. He opened the driver's door and climbed into his seat.

"We're a go, then, madam?"

"Yes, Mr. Pibb, we're a go."

He gave the horn a little tap to alert Kat, who beeped back.

"Shall we go, then?"

"Yes," she said, giving Lucifer a scratch under his chin, "but I have a law in mind, Mr. Pibb."

"A law, madam? I thought that was *my* territory."

"Well, indulge me this once, Mr. Pibb. I'm thinking of the Cruise Law."

"What?" he said, then snapped his fingers and laughed.

"Yes, Mr. Pibb."

"*You feel the need . . .*"

"*The need for speed.*"

Mr. Pibb laughed, pulled the limo away from the curb, and accelerated into traffic, Kat quickly speeding by, setting a furious pace.

Luna stared out the window, tears glistening, drops of rain splashing on the window and streaking sideways as Mr. Pibb picked up speed. Scotland was miles and miles away, but with the heavy cloud cover, it seemed like they could already be there.

Lucifer purred in agreement.

67

Office of Detective Chief Inspector Roger Falvey, Scotland Yard, Saturday Morning, October 22.

Detective Inspector Harry Morton sat across the desk from his superior, trying his best not to leap out of his chair and slam his fist down to protest the nonsense pouring out of Falvey's mouth.

Falvey agreed that Harry and Detective Sergeant Kadika had foiled the plot to abduct Luna, but at too high a cost in Falvey's opinion. *Nonsense,* Harry thought.

"Sir," he began, trying to interrupt, but Falvey just shook his head.

"No, you just sit there and listen," Falvey said, jabbing a finger at him. "One, you should have *never* authorized firearms."

"But sir—"

"Two, you should have waited for me before issuing orders of *any* kind. You *knew* I would only be delayed a few minutes."

Harry straightened himself, fists clenched.

"Three, you should have waited for backup before engaging those men."

"Bollocks, there was no time!" Harry shouted at Falvey. "They'd have had her for sure."

"You don't know that, and sit yourself down! Four, *Four*, Kadika is dead because of you, as well as the man who could have led us to whomever was behind the attempted abduction."

"That's not fair!"

"Five, the media are having a right field day over that video made by Ms. Fearnow's photographer—it's all over the internet and the telly."

"So that's what this is all about? You're fucking embarrassed, is that it?"

Falvey glowered at him. "It shows Kadika lopping off the head of a man with a machete—a *machete* for God's sake. Of course, it's embarrassing. It's ludicrous!"

"It was personal, sir, personal and fitting. The man had killed Kadika's sister, probably with that same machete."

Falvey held up his hand. "Enough, enough!"

Harry slumped back down in his chair, wondering whether he should just resign and be done with it all. That's where Falvey seemed to be headed, so why the hell fight it.

"Is there a six, sir?"

Falvey slammed his hand on the desk. "Don't be impertinent, Morton. And yes, there is a six. Six, that video makes us look like bunglers and the supposed victims like superheroes."

Harry had to admit that possibility. He had fired his weapon several times, and Kadika, that gentle giant of a man, had taken out the main man, but it was Luna Fearnow, her friend and fellow model Kat Murphy, and her chauffeur, Pontius Pibb, who had won the day. Their actions had been nothing short of incredible.

Harry shook his head, then nodded. "So it appears, although in our defense, the photographer was Luna's photographer— she was there for a photo shoot—so it's only natural that the man would focus on her and her friends, and not on us."

Harry's admission seemed to make Falvey back down a bit. He slumped back in his chair, his hands dropping to his lap.

"Harry," he said after a moment, "I know you were trying to do the right thing, but to the outside world, your actions appeared dangerous and inappropriate. Some characterized your actions as going rogue."

"Rogue?"

"I know that's not true. However, there will be an inquiry."

Here it comes, Harry thought. "So, I'm to be suspended, then?"

Falvey shook his head. "As tempting as that is, no. I have other plans for you."

"Oh, and what might that be?"

Falvey opened a folder on the top of his desk, which was otherwise perfectly empty, quite unlike Harry's messy desk.

"Did you see the creature they found up at Loch Ness, the Little Nessie?"

"Yes, on the telly. Do you think it's truly a baby Nessie?"

"They thought so at first, but now a scientist, a marine biologist on the Loch Ness Project, says absolutely not."

"Really? Then what is it?"

"That's the interesting thing. It seems to have sprouted wings and is growing at an alarming rate. They think it's — well, they think it's a dragon."

Harry straightened and leaned forward in his chair. "The green dragon. It's the Darwin story playing out, just like he said in his journal. If our dragon-man, Jamie Doyle, saw the story, he'll be headed for Scotland right now, to kill that dragon, or be killed by it."

"Precisely," said Falvey. "I've been on the telephone with Inverness, and they've agreed to work with us on apprehending him and dealing with this dragon, if that's what it is. You need to pack a bag and head north as soon as possible. We've booked you a flight."

Harry was already racing for the door.

"Wait!" Falvey shouted. "You'll need this folder—the boarding pass."

Harry turned back, snatched the folder out of Falvey's hand, and was gone, the door slamming loudly behind him.

Falvey slumped back into his chair again and let out a heavy sigh. He had planned to confront Harry about his obvious affection for Ms. Fearnow, a rumor that was more than widespread throughout the department, but he had decided not to. The reassignment to Scotland would accomplish the goal, keeping Harry and Ms. Fearnow apart.

The whole sorry incident should never have gone down the way it did, he thought. *But that's what happens when an officer thinks with his cock and not his head.*

68

London Midland Train, en Route to Inverness, Saturday Morning, October 22.

Jamie sat next to the window in first class, peering out at the English countryside. Li and Peng had gone to the dining car, leaving him alone with his thoughts. *The Green Dragon.*

According to Li's so-called manual, it would be a fearsome creature, even as small as it was now. Jamie thought otherwise. He would quickly dispatch it, and then they would be on their way to somewhere to wait for the emergence of yet another dragon. This should all go quickly. He *would* be a god.

He would have to consult the manual on the other dragons, of course, but right now, he seemed content to stare out the window and think about his kills. He seemed to enjoy each more than the last. *Bruce thought he could outrun me. Ha! He could still hear the cracking of Bruce's bones and the look on the face of the security guard. Priceless.*

He saw from the reflection in the window that someone had sat down opposite him. A woman. A beautiful woman in rose-colored aviator glasses, very sexy, tall and athletic, well over six feet tall, with short-cropped black hair and skin like alabaster. She was wearing knee-high red boots that accentuated her long legs, and a short sleeveless white dress with a pattern of black lines forming small squares. A red suede jacket was draped over one well-toned arm.

He couldn't help admiring her stunning figure, and there was something about her perfume, a scent that seemed familiar somehow.

"I'm sorry, miss," he said, "but that seat is taken, I'm afraid."

The woman seemed confused. "Oh, excuse me."

She started to rise.

"Wait," Jamie said. "I'd much rather talk to you than the gentleman who occupies that seat. I'll get him to take another one, assuming that would be all right with you."

She smiled and sat back down. "That would be wonderful. I was so looking forward to a good conversation on this trip."

"Are you headed for Inverness by chance?"

"Why, yes, I am."

Wonderful, thought Jamie. *Wonderful*. He reached out his hand. "My name is Jamie."

She took his hand and smiled. "Call me Lily."

EPILOGUE

The Dog and Bear, Lenham, Kent, Wednesday, April 26, 1882, 12:35 a.m.

Lily jumped down from the carriage and moved quickly into the inn, waving off the proprietor, who asked whether she would like a late meal or libation, and then proceeded to her room, locking the door behind her and dumping the notebooks on the bed.

She sat down and sorted them. Six notebooks began with the letter L for Lilly, and the mysterious seventh notebook was marked B-1. A chill went through her. *B for brother?*

She opened the notebook, Darwin's familiar handwriting filling the pages. Her heart leaped when she saw that the notebook was addressed to her.

My dearest Lily,
   I have for some time wondered about your brother, and how he might differ from you in terms of strength, abilities, and intelligence. Would he be more dragonlike than you? More fierce after transforming? Would he have your intelligence and cunning?
   The key in all this, it seems to me, is you and your brother's manner of birth, you from an egg (I must say, it

still seems impossible to me, and yet it is true) and your brother coming into the world from a live birth.

You will remember my studies of that tiny little barnacle I called Mr. Arthrobalanus and which is better known as cryptophalus minutus. It is this little barnacle, the same kind that encrusted your egg, that has revealed a clue, I think. It seems to have a curious habit, the ability to change its host to its own ends. So, in a real way, and admittedly a strange way, you are both children of Mr. Arthrobalanus. But each in a different way. So, this is my theory, what I suspect about your brother, and if I am right, what you must know—and heed—at your very peril before you face him . . . ."

ABOUT THE AUTHOR

Len Boswell is the author of fifteen additional books, including the award-winning *Simon Grave Mysteries*. He lives in the mountains of West Virginia with his wife, Ruth, and their two dogs, Cinder and Daisy, a speedy rat terrier and a beagle who doubles as a paper shredder.

NOTE FROM THE AUTHOR

Word-of-mouth is crucial for any author to succeed. If you enjoyed *The Barnacle's Son*, please leave a review online—anywhere you are able. Even if it's just a sentence or two. It would make all the difference and would be very much appreciated.

Thanks!

Len

We hope you enjoyed reading this title from:

BLACK ROSE
writing™

www.blackrosewriting.com

Subscribe to our mailing list – *The Rosevine* – and receive **FREE** books, daily deals, and stay current with news about upcoming releases and our hottest authors.
Scan the QR code below to sign up.

Already a subscriber? Please accept a sincere thank you for being a fan of Black Rose Writing authors.

View other Black Rose Writing titles at
www.blackrosewriting.com/books and use promo code
PRINT to receive a **20% discount** when purchasing.